THE CASE OF THE
PHANTOM TREASURE

THE CASE OF THE PHANTOM TREASURE

NICK SHERIDAN
ILLUSTRATED BY DAVID O'CONNELL

SIMON & SCHUSTER

First published in Great Britain in 2023 by Simon & Schuster UK Ltd

1 3 5 7 9 10 8 6 4 2

Simon & Schuster UK Ltd
1st Floor, 222 Gray's Inn Road
London WC1X 8HB

www.simonandschuster.co.uk
www.simonandschuster.com.au
www.simonandschuster.co.in

Simon & Schuster Australia, Sydney
Simon & Schuster India, New Delhi

A CIP catalogue record for this book
is available from the British Library.

PB ISBN 978-1-3985-0687-9
eBook ISBN 978-1-3985-0688-6
eAudio ISBN 978-1-3985-0689-3

Typeset in Garamond by M Rules
Printed and bound in the UK using 100% renewable
electricity at CPI Group (UK) Ltd

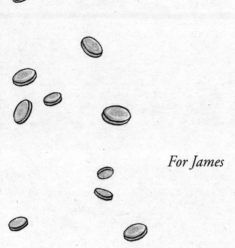

For James

PROLOGUE

1723

Captain Horatio Huxley hauled himself up to the crow's nest and wrapped an arm round the ship's mast, shielding his eyes from the rain and wind that whipped through the sails and threatened to blow him overboard.

Scanning the horizon, which was shrouded by dark clouds and split by streaks of lightning, Huxley pulled a sodden clump of parchment from his overcoat. What had once been a map of the way home now resembled a damp rag that had been used to wipe up an oil spill. He tossed it into the wind with a snarl.

'Make a U-turn!' came a voice from his shoulder.

'Shut it, Mosey!' snapped Huxley. The parrot squawked back in indignation. 'If it weren't for you,' he bellowed over the screaming wind, 'we'd be sitting in front of a roaring fire, bellies full of roast pheasant and hot cocoa!'

'At the roundabout, take the second exit!' Mosey screeched.

'We're in the middle of the ocean!' Huxley roared. 'There are no roundabouts here!'

'Make a U-turn!' Mosey cried again. 'Make a U-turn!'

The ship suddenly gave a violent lurch, and Huxley hugged the mast even tighter. The *Captain's Revenge* was being tossed like a rag doll back and forth, enormous waves battering her from every direction. Somewhere far below, Huxley heard a tremendous *crunch* as the ocean gnawed away at the ship's hull – she wouldn't hold up much longer in this storm.

Huxley looked down and saw his first mate staggering across the deck, spluttering against the sheets of rain pummelling the ship.

'Damage report, Podge!' Huxley barked down at him.

Podge caught hold of the mast and hung on tight.

'I'm soaked, cap'n!' he called up. 'I think I sprained my ankle, the scurvy is making my teeth fall out, I've lost the feeling in my toes and I can feel a migraine coming on!'

'The ship, Podge!' roared Huxley. 'A damage report for the ship, you gilly-livered greasepot!'

'Oh ... We're sinking!' called back Podge. 'The hull, bow, keel, galley, bridge, hold, stern and amidships are all underwater!'

'Good grief!' shouted Huxley. 'That's almost the entire ship! What about the poop deck?'

'The poop deck is fine, but it smells awful! Permission to panic, cap'n?'

'Pull yourself together, Podge!' commanded Huxley. 'Ready the lifeboats.'

'Oh, I knew I forgot something. They're underwater too, cap'n!'

Huxley growled and spat out a mouthful of rain. On his shoulder, Mosey was still giving directions.

'Take the next right, then join the motorway!'

'What's the satnav saying, cap'n?' shouted up Podge.

'It's on the blink!' Huxley yelled back. 'It thinks we're on a motorway.'

'Speed cameras ahead!' squawked Mosey.

Huxley pulled up his collar round his face and tried to think of a plan. He wasn't ready to let the *Captain's Revenge* sink to the black depths of the sea, taking him, his crew and their precious cargo with her.

'We've come too far to give up now, Podge!' he yelled down to his first mate. 'We found the treasure, and we're going to bring it home!'

Suddenly, there came a tremendous sound, as if the sky itself was being ripped apart.

Podge checked the seat of his trousers. 'I think my breeches have just split,' he cried.

'Idiot!' Huxley pointed upwards. 'It's the sail!'

The wind had sheared the sail of the *Captain's Revenge* into rags. It whipped away and disappeared into the frothing ocean below.

'Permission to panic now, cap'n?' Podge called up to the crow's nest.

Huxley sighed down at his first mate, then raised his hand to his temple in a stiff navy salute. 'Permission granted, Podge. We're going down.'

'Thank you, cap'n.' Podge returned the salute, then screeched in terror and ran from the deck.

Huxley watched him go sourly. 'It's just you and me now, Mosey,' he growled to the parrot.

Huxley thought of the treasure he'd found, now hidden deep in the belly of the ship. Would the riches end up like him and his men, lost to the sea? Would they ever be found? The thought lit an angry glow in his chest, and he screwed his hands into fists.

'I swear this, Mosey!' he shouted to his parrot over the crashing of the waves. 'No one will ever take my treasure from me! Anyone who finds this ship will wish they'd never even laid eyes on it!' Captain Horatio Huxley looked out over the heaving ocean before him, his mouth a grim slash of determination. 'That's a promise!'

CHAPTER ONE

Present Day

Olly Rudd pulled a pair of binoculars from his rucksack and scanned the shoreline of Bony Beach. He and Riz Sekhon had been waiting on the sand for almost an hour, watching the distant trees for any sign of their friends arriving.

Drew and Anton Hill lived at the newly named Snoops Bay Academy, high in the hills above the town. Until last summer, that very same academy had been the lair of Madame Sigourney Strang and her vicious gang of sausage dogs. The four children had managed to rid the town of Strang and her dastardly scheme to brainwash the entire population, and a new owner had taken command of the boarding school. Anton insisted the food was just as cold and lumpy as it had been when Strang was in charge, but his older brother, Drew, was quick to remind him that it was a small price to pay for not having a crazy beautician trying to turn them into zombies. Anton grudgingly agreed.

As the months had stretched on, Riz and Olly found themselves spending more and more time with the Hill brothers. They'd become used to Drew's mood swings and his stubbornness and had grown to admire his fierce protectiveness of his brother. As much as the Hills bickered, and occasionally resorted to wrestling each other to the ground in fits of rage, it was clear how much they depended on each other.

Neither Olly nor Riz had ever brought up the subject of the Hill brothers' parents – or rather, their apparent lack of them. They'd never even properly spoken about how the Hills had ended up at the academy in the first place. Both Riz and Olly could sense that neither brother was ready for that conversation.

Olly lowered the binoculars – there was still no sign of Drew and Anton. To pass the time, he decided to discuss potential new articles for next month's edition of *Unearthed*, his beloved muck magazine. Riz immediately shut down the idea.

'No way!' she groaned as Olly began to pitch his article about a Belgian artist who used llama dung instead of paint. 'When I was *paid* to be your friend, I had to listen to stories about sludge, but I refuse to do it for free!'

Olly lapsed into silence, a small smile creeping across his face. Riz had just admitted they were *real* friends now, and that his parents were no longer paying her to hang out with him. Riz had gradually begun to wind down her Fake Friend business since last summer. In fact, Olly hadn't seen her advertise her services for months.

He suddenly jumped to his feet, squinting into the dunes. 'I see them!'

Riz raised her head and frowned. 'Did they bring sandwiches?'

Drew and Anton had appeared over the dunes, and as they drew closer, the sound of their voices grew louder. They seemed to be in the midst of a heated discussion.

'I'm saying a starfish has three legs and two arms!'

Drew barked at his brother as he pulled his rucksack from his back and flopped down onto the sand beside Riz. 'And that's the end of it!'

'A starfish *obviously* has two legs and three arms!' Anton insisted. 'And a brain about the size of yours!'

'Brotherly love in action.' Riz bumped her knuckles against Drew's closed fist and eyed the rucksack. 'Please tell me you've got sandwiches in there?'

Anton loomed over his brother, his hands on his hips and a disapproving glare on his face. 'We *did* bring sandwiches,' he told Riz. 'But *someone* got peckish on the way here and scoffed the lot!'

Riz wailed in despair. 'DREW!' she whined. 'I only agreed to come because I thought there'd be sandwiches.'

Olly raised an eyebrow and cleared his throat loudly.

'And *obviously* for an *Unearthed* mud-finding mission,' added Riz quickly. '*Twenty Muds, Silts, Sands and Clays You Wouldn't Expect to Find in Snoops Bay.* Isn't that right, Olly?'

'Correct, Riz!' Olly nodded approvingly. 'You keep this up and I might promote you to deputy editor!'

Riz looked horrified.

Anton turned away from his friends and surveyed

their surroundings. 'It's not exactly what I imagined,' he muttered. 'I thought there'd be more to look at . . .'

Anton was right. Bony Beach was deserted. A grey and mournful stretch of shoreline, it was mostly avoided by the residents of Snoops Bay and the tourists who came to visit the town. Other beaches around the bay had names like Pleasure Strand, Ha-Ha Hamlet and Calm Cove. No one knew where the name Bony Beach had come from, but there were old tales and ghost stories of pirate bones buried deep in the sand. And it was said that on a quiet night, you could hear the distant moans of seamen trying to claw their way to the surface.

The beach was curved into a crescent, a lonely inlet fringed on all sides by steep dunes topped with skeletal trees. Their branches were empty of birds and waved sadly in the breeze, a long row of accusing fingers rising to meet the ominous clouds above. The air was cold and almost sour, and the wind never seemed to stop howling in from the sea across the sand. It was a spooky place.

'This is where you'll find the rare stuff, my little muck apprentices!' Olly declared, plopping himself onto the sand and carefully unpacking his muck kit.

Riz, Drew and Anton watched dubiously as he laid out his tools, most of them spattered with muck and dirt in various shades. There were jars, test tubes, tape measures, a spade, a bag of rods in different shapes and sizes, a magnifying glass, a sieve (that looked suspiciously like the one Olly's mum owned) and a battered old manual that seemed to have gone through a few cycles in a washing machine. Across its cover were the words: *Mud is Thicker Than Water: A Muck-Hunter's Journey.*

And so their afternoon unfolded: digging and gathering samples from the cold and gritty ground of Bony Beach. Riz, Drew and Anton had no idea what they were looking for (Riz had hoped to spend most of the afternoon shoving sandwiches into her mouth), so they resorted to picking random patches of earth and digging in the hope of unearthing something remotely interesting.

Drew kept an itemized list of the objects they found. It made for sorry reading:

One copy of the Snoops Bay Sniffer from 1989
One seagull feather
One jar of pickled onions (empty)
One baby's nappy (full)
One bottle of sun cream, extra thick (half full/
    half empty, depending on your outlook)

And that was it.

Olly, meanwhile, was having a ball. Every spadeful of mud he shovelled out of the earth, he decanted into a jar, examined, labelled and stowed away in his rucksack. In the space of a few short hours, he'd bagged himself fresh samples of Saltsilt, Worm's Delight and Spanish Sodclod. These would now be brought back to his bedroom for a thorough forensic investigation, which he estimated would take weeks.

Olly was just packing away the last of his jars when Drew and Anton came racing down the beach. Anton was clutching something small and shiny in his hand.

'Look!' Drew yelled as they lurched to a halt, showering a protesting Riz with sand.

'What is that?' Olly squinted. 'Is it a bottle?'

'Sure is. And it's got a message in it!' Anton crowed in delight, crouching down on the sand and yanking the cork from the mouth of the bottle.

Olly squinted over his shoulder. There *was* a damp piece of paper rolled up inside. A thrill of excitement shuddered down his spine.

'Well, let's hear it!' Riz had paused her digging, popping her head up like a meerkat.

'Read it out, Anton!' Olly cried.

A solemn hush fell over the group, with only the whistling breeze to fill the silence. Anton poked his finger into the neck of the bottle and carefully pulled out the paper, making sure not to tear it. He handed the bottle to Drew, who grinned as his brother unfolded the message.

Anton's eyebrows shot upwards, his mouth falling

open in a little 'o' of surprise. He looked from the message to Olly, then back to the message again. 'It can't be!' he gasped.

'What?' Olly squeaked. 'What does it say?'

'It's . . . ' Anton paused. 'It's . . . for you, Olly!'

'For me?' Olly's voice was barely more than a whisper.

Anton held out the message with trembling hands. Olly plucked it from his fingers and looked down at it, screwing his eyes almost shut. He took a deep breath and read the message: WE'RE BORED.

Furious, Olly poked Anton in the ribs. Anton in turn darted out of his reach and high-fived his brother in fits of laughter.

'Hang on, I think I've found something too!' Riz tried to get their attention.

Anton flopped onto the sand, still giggling. 'Is it a note that says, "Can we go home now?"' Olly glowered at him.

'NO, I'VE REALLY FOUND SOMETHING!' Riz yelled, beginning to scrabble at the sand.

Anton and Drew stopped giggling, and the three boys turned to look at Riz. She was crouched down in front of a small mound, scratching at a small, dark patch on the side. Her fingers scraped across something hard, and she gently brushed away the clumps of damp earth clinging to her find.

Olly appeared over her shoulder. 'Gently, Riz. Gently!' He thrust a tiny brush into her hand. 'Use the excavation instrument!'

'Olly, this is a pastry brush from your mum's kitchen cabinet.' Riz rolled her eyes. 'Should we really be using it to dig through muck?'

'Mum's sausage rolls *were* a little bit gritty yesterday,' Olly admitted. 'But it's the best way to obtain a full specimen!'

Riz reluctantly took the pastry brush and began to lightly dust sand off the mound in front of her.

'It's a plank of wood.' Anton broke the silence.

'It's two planks of wood,' corrected Drew.

'Three!' squeaked Olly in disbelief.

'What on earth ...' Riz muttered, brushing harder and harder.

She was slowly but surely clearing sand off row after row of planks, nailed together in a gentle curve, like the ribcage of a huge sea creature buried for centuries under the sand. Olly, Drew and Anton began to help, clearing handfuls of sand away from the discovery, which seemed to stretch in every direction. No one spoke, the air filling instead with the sound of scraping and their excited panting.

Finally, the friends stopped and sat back so they could take a proper look at what they'd uncovered. It was the belly of an enormous ship, warped and rotting from being soaked in seawater for hundreds of years. The vessel seemed to have been lying on its side when it was burried, and they'd only managed to uncover a tiny portion of the base, with armies of limpets clinging to the rotting wood.

'Riz,' Olly said, his eyes wide. 'This is incredible!'

Riz could hardly believe what they were seeing. 'How old do you think it is?' she asked.

Olly pulled some jars from his rucksack eagerly. 'I'm going to collect samples and find out. The muck and seaweed around the ship should give us a clue. But if I was to guess from the texture and colour ...' He scrunched up his face in concentration. 'I'd say ... two hundred years old?'

'Three hundred!' came Drew's voice. 'It's three hundred years old.'

Olly and Riz looked at their friend in surprise. 'And how are you calculating that, Drew?' Olly asked, peering over his glasses. 'Do you have a secret superpower for ageing muck that I don't know about?'

'No, smarty-pants.' Drew pointed towards the ship. 'It says it right there.'

Olly and Riz followed the direction of his finger. Sure enough, a rotting old board nailed to the side of the ship answered Riz's question.

'1723,' Riz read aloud. 'The *Captain's Revenge*.' Her mouth hung open in shock. 'It's been buried here for *three hundred years*!'

Drew gazed at the sign, seemingly lost in thought. 'It

must have been a navy ship,' he guessed.

'I'm not so sure,' Anton interrupted, appearing beside his brother. He'd continued digging around the ship while the others had been marvelling over the discovery. In his hands now was a ragged curtain of black fabric, blotched with sea-salt stains. He dropped it in front of the group. 'Look at this flag.'

Olly, Riz and Drew looked down at what Anton had found. Then they looked at each other. Then back down to the flag again. A toothy skull was leering up at them.

'Uh-oh,' whispered Riz.

'Is that what I think it is?' Olly muttered.

'It sure is,' said Riz. 'That's a Jolly Roger.' She looked up grimly at her pals. 'This was a pirate ship.'

CHAPTER TWO

Captain Jasper Brandish thwacked a huge sea trout onto his chopping board and frowned at the four children standing before him.

'Why are you interested in pirates?' he rasped.

'It's for a school project!' Riz repeated, nervously glancing at the fish, which stared back with blank indifference.

Brandish grunted, unconvinced. 'Smells fishy to me!'

'Well, there is a trout right in front of you!' piped up Anton, earning himself a prod in the ribs from Drew.

'Look, kids, I'm busy right now,' growled Brandish.

The Red Herring Fish Emporium, Snoops Bay's only fishmonger, was heaving with customers, all desperately trying to catch the attention of Captain Brandish. It was rumoured that he had once made a living as a pirate, and he certainly liked their style. Under a bright yellow fisherman's coat, he wore a crumpled linen shirt with a patterned waistcoat and a kerchief knotted round his neck. Below a length of thick fishing line that he used as a belt were a set of knee-length breeches, socks pulled up to his calves, and a pair of black buckled boots. A woollen cap was perched jauntily on his fiery red hair, matching the frizzy whiskers that snaked down past his ears. He often walked with a limp, though the affected leg seemed to change regularly, according to the more observant residents of Snoops Bay.

The Red Herring Fish Emporium was scarcely bigger than a bedroom, and everywhere the children looked, fish stared back. A long ice cabinet lined one entire wall of the shop, displaying Brandish's goods: neat white fillets of cod, repulsive-looking monkfish, majestic sea bass and icy mountains of bream, pollock, haddock and hake. Shelves groaned under the weight of tinned tuna, sardines, anchovies and mackerel. And the entire back wall was stacked high with bubbling water tanks, filled to the brim with wriggling lobsters, bright red crabs, oysters, clams and even a grumpy-looking octopus. Unsurprisingly, the place reeked of fish.

'Twenty rock oysters please, Mr Brandish,' barked an imperious-looking woman in an enormous fur coat.

'That's *Captain* Brandish to you!' growled the fishmonger over the counter.

'Excuse me, *Captain Brandish*.' An older gentleman elbowed his way to the front. 'I'm still waiting on my swordfish.'

'You'll wait as long as it takes, you bilge-sucking, lily-livered landlubber!' barked the captain, shaking the trout threateningly in the gentleman's direction.

'We heard you had experience in the field of piracy?' Olly cut in, keeping well out of the way of the trout. 'My dad told me you're an expert.'

Brandish grunted as he wrapped the trout in a shroud of brown paper and tossed it over the counter to a waiting customer. 'I've seen my fair share of salty dogs,' he told them.

'I thought you only sold fish?' said Anton.

Brandish dug into a mountain of oysters with a scoop and poured a few mounds into a paper bag. 'Oysters!' he shouted at the woman in the fur coat. 'Thank you, Mrs Turbot. Give my best to the mayor!'

As Mrs Turbot grabbed the bag of oysters and stuffed a wad of notes into Brandish's outstretched hand, Riz tried to catch his attention.

'So you're a pirate?' she asked.

He shrugged. 'I'm on a career break,' he said and slammed the till shut with a *zing*. 'It's not a great way to earn a living, if I'm honest. No pension plan, no perks, and you do get bored of plundering after a while.'

'We found a ship!' Drew called over the din. 'We think it might be a . . .'

'My *swordfish*!' called the older gentleman again.

'*ALL RIGHT!*' roared Brandish. He reached into his ice cabinet and pulled out a whole swordfish, its eyes frozen open in surprise.

As quick as a cat, Brandish leapt out from behind the counter, swiping the fish at the customer. The nose of the swordfish cut cleanly through the man's braces with two loud rips, and the poor customer squealed in horror as his trousers collapsed round his ankles.

The entire fishmonger's burst into spontaneous applause, and Brandish lowered the swordfish with an extravagant flourish.

'Walk the plank, you brine-brained scallywag!' he commanded.

'What do you mean?' cried the older gentleman, trying to yank his trousers up over his underpants.

'Get out of my shop!' Brandish snapped as he tossed the swordfish back into the cabinet and slammed it shut. 'Who's next?'

'We only want to ask you a few questions,' Olly pleaded as the customers surged forward, threatening to flatten him against the counter.

'I'm afraid not, boy,' barked Brandish. 'I haven't time to be wagging tongues. This is my busiest time of year!'

'We found a ship on Bony Beach called the *Captain's Revenge*!' Olly shouted.

There was a deafening crash, and the entire shop jumped in fright. Brandish had dropped an entire tray of prawns all over the floor.

'What did you say?' he croaked.

Olly threw a glance at Riz and gulped. 'We found a ship ...'

Brandish leant towards Olly until his whiskers were almost brushing the tip of his nose. 'Did you say you found the *Captain's Revenge*?'

Another gulp from Olly, followed by a nod. Brandish slowly straightened up and cleared his throat.

'Everybody out!' he announced. 'We're closed!'

CHAPTER THREE

Brandish flipped the sign on the shop door from OPEN to CLOSED and led the friends upstairs to what he called the 'captain's quarters'. As they climbed the rickety stairs, Olly puffed under the weight of his mud kit (he'd eagerly shovelled several spadefuls of the stuff from underneath the *Captain's Revenge* into his biggest jar).

Brandish kicked open the front door of his flat with a loud bang and ushered them inside. Once their eyes adjusted to the gloom, they found themselves in a low-ceilinged parlour, lined on all sides by rows and rows of crooked bookshelves. Piles of leather-bound books and mountains of curling parchment were stuffed into every nook and cranny, lit by the yellow light of dozens of candles. The whole place was a bonfire waiting to happen.

Everything was caked with dust too – the books, the

carpet, the framed pictures, even the curtains. There wasn't a single square inch uncovered. In the centre of the room sat an enormous round table, sagging under the weight of more books, ledgers and captain's logbooks.

Brandish limped over to a tiny gas stove tucked under a pile of saucepans and spread his arms out wide. 'Welcome to the captain's quarters!' he told them. 'Are you peckish?'

'I'm starving!' sighed Riz with relief. 'What have you got?'

'Fish-head soup!' Brandish beamed.

'Oh ... actually, I'm stuffed,' said Riz quickly. 'We ate at the beach.'

A sudden bubbling sound came from a cabinet behind Drew, who yelped in fright and dashed behind his brother. 'What was that?' he gasped.

Brandish gave a chuckle. 'Oh, don't mind Kourtney. She's harmless!'

He elbowed his way past Drew and pulled the cabinet open. The group watched nervously as he reached into the darkness and lifted out a huge fishbowl, placing it precariously on top of the nearest tower of books.

Anton took a careful step towards the bowl and peered inside. 'Is that ... snot?' he asked eventually.

Brandish shushed him quickly. 'Don't let her hear you say that! She's very sensitive about her appearance.'

Riz peered into the fishbowl. Kourtney stared back.

'She's a blobfish!' announced Brandish.

It was immediately obvious how Kourtney the blobfish had earned her name. Sat in the murky water of the fishbowl was a solid mass of pinkish jelly with an enormous sagging nose under two mournful eyes. Her mouth was turned down in a sad pout as she gazed miserably up at the children.

'She looks pretty sad,' muttered Riz.

'Wouldn't you, if you looked like that?' giggled Drew.

Brandish whipped out a tube of bright orange fish food from his coat and tipped some crumbs into the bowl. Kourtney ignored them, burping a few lonely bubbles while seeming to give an exasperated sigh.

'I won her in a game of chance, thirty years ago when I was just a cabin

boy.' Brandish peered down into the fishbowl and gave the glass a fond rub. 'Beat an old pirate called Slippery Sid at Twister. Isn't she a beauty?'

'Erm . . . sure.' Olly nodded.

'She's very rare,' Brandish continued. 'She's over forty years old, and she swam all the way here from the Raging Reef off the coast of the Galápagos Islands!'

Olly's eyebrows shot up. 'I have a jar of muck from the Raging Reef!' he squeaked. 'It's said to be made of ninety per cent pirate bones!'

'Well, I hope you have it under lock and key, boy,' Brandish told him gravely. 'Like Kourtney here, that muck is priceless.'

'It's in my secret treasure box in my back garden,' Olly told him.

'It won't be a secret if you tell everyone where it is, Olly.' Riz tutted.

'Anyway,' said Brandish loudly, giving the round table a whack with his open palm. 'You didn't come here to pay Kourtney a visit. Tell me what you found on Bony Beach.'

The group explained what had happened. When they finished, they noticed Brandish was gazing deeply into Kourtney's fishbowl, seemingly lost in thought.

A dark expression had clouded his face when Anton mentioned the black flag emblazoned with the skull and crossbones.

'Well, sink me!' he muttered.

'We thought you might know where the ship came from,' Riz suggested weakly. 'We heard sailing is your hobby.'

'Hobby?' Brandish suddenly snapped, drawing himself up to his full height and giving a sweeping salute. 'Young lady, you're looking at one of the last surviving pirates in Britain!'

Riz and Olly exchanged a doubtful glance.

'So you're an actual pirate . . . ?' asked Olly.

Brandish huffed and limped over to a framed certificate hanging above his stove. He yanked it off the wall, blew an enormous cloud of dust off it and thrust it at Riz. She squinted at it in the gloom and then read aloud the dark red scrawl printed on it:

'This certificate is awarded to Captain Jasper Brandish, Esquire, in recognition of his dedication to piracy in all its forms, and for outstanding achievements in Hijacking, Smuggling, Arson, Looting, Ungentlemanly Conduct and General Depravity.'

'What kind of ink is that?' asked Olly, eyeing the red

font nervously. 'It looks a lot like bloo—'

'Beetroot juice,' Brandish quickly interrupted as he snatched the certificate back. 'Piracy is a lot more than a hobby for me,' he told Riz sternly. 'The Pirate Association doesn't hand those certificates out to just anyone. They literally *can't* hand them out – their president has hooks for hands!'

'So why are you running a fishmonger in Snoops Bay?' asked Anton suddenly.

Brandish sniffed and placed the certificate carefully back in its place. 'I told you. I'm on an extended career break,' he said. 'Kourtney hasn't been well lately, and I'm her full-time carer.'

Kourtney blew some bubbles sadly.

Brandish whipped back round to face the children. 'But I know of the *Captain's Revenge*. There isn't a pirate living or dead who hasn't heard of it, and its captain.'

At that very moment, a chill wind seemed to flutter through the room, the candles flickering in the sudden breeze.

'What happened to them?' asked Drew in a hushed voice.

Brandish looked grim. 'The *Captain's Revenge* sailed

for twenty years under the command of Captain Horatio Huxley, one of the most dangerous pirates who ever lived.'

He limped over to the table and began sifting through mountains of parchment. 'He was a naval officer who let greed take over his mind. He and his crew travelled around the globe, capturing every ship they came across and plundering treasure from here to Timbuktu. It was said that any sailor who saw the *Captain's Revenge* coming over the horizon immediately made themselves walk the plank, rather than look into the eyes of the dastardly Captain Huxley!' Brandish flipped open a thick leather tome and pointed to a yellowed ink drawing. 'There he is.'

Riz, Olly, Drew and Anton crowded around the book and peered down at the drawing. It was a full-page illustration of a man standing on the deck of a ship, waving a cutlass threateningly at the sky with a cruel smile on his face. He was wrapped head-to-toe in black, his heavy overcoat billowing wildly in the sea wind, and a pirate captain's hat sat upon a messy nest of dark hair.

'He doesn't seem like a particularly friendly individual,' murmured Olly over Riz's shoulder.

'You can say that again.' Brandish shivered, clamping the book shut. 'Huxley terrorized the seven seas all his life, until ...'

There was a pause. 'Until what?' squeaked Anton.

A dark shadow passed over Brandish's face again. 'October the thirtieth, 1723. The last voyage of the *Captain's Revenge*. Huxley had spent the previous two years obsessively searching the globe for some great lost treasure, and he found it.'

'What treasure?' Anton screeched even higher.

'That, boy, is a mystery,' said Brandish sadly. 'The *Captain's Revenge*, and the treasure, never made it to shore. Huxley and his crew ran into some bad squalls about a hundred miles from port and were sent down to Davy Jones's Locker.'

'That means the bottom of the ocean,' Drew muttered to Anton.

'I know what it means!' Anton shot back before mouthing to Riz, 'No, I didn't.'

'Apparently Huxley's parrot gave him the wrong directions,' Brandish went on. 'That's the rumour anyway. The only survivor was the first mate – an idiot by the name of Podge. He trod water for two days after the ship went down, until a colony of seals mistook him for one of their own and adopted him. He was discovered three years later on a deserted island, flopping around and clapping with the animals. When the doctors finally got some sense from him, he told them what had happened. But the ship, and the treasure, were never found.'

'Until today!' gasped Riz, feeling her face beginning to flush with excitement.

'Until today,' agreed Brandish, sinking into a squashy chair by the wall. The shadows cast by the candles danced across his face.

'But . . .' he said softly. 'There's something else you should know.'

The children waited. 'Yes?' prompted Drew in an anxious voice.

Brandish fixed them with a grim gaze. 'You may wish you'd never found that ship,' he said in little more than a whisper. 'For it's cursed.'

Silence enveloped the room, broken only by the sound of Kourtney burping a trail of bubbles.

'Cursed?' repeated Riz. 'What do you mean?'

'I mean there's a curse on that ship,' said Brandish. 'A terrible curse that will befall the poor souls who found it.'

Drew snorted. 'Rubbish! You're pulling our legs.'

But Brandish wasn't smiling. 'It's no laughing matter, boy. Podge the pirate recounted how on the stormy night the ship sank, Huxley swore that whoever uncovered it and the treasure would pay a terrible price.'

Riz glanced at the boys, whose faces had turned a milky-white colour.

'But . . .' she stammered. 'That would be . . . us!'

'Indeed, it would.' Brandish sat in silence as the four children gaped at him in disbelief. The candles flickered again, and the room suddenly felt icy cold.

'So, what's going to happen to us?' asked Anton in a high voice.

Brandish shrugged. 'Who knows? Perhaps it's just an old pirates' tale.' His face darkened again. 'Or perhaps it's not. A week after Podge was found, he escaped from the hospital and flopped back into the ocean to find his seal family. When they discovered he was gone, they saw a message scratched on the wall of his room. A poem.'

'A poem?' Riz gulped. 'What did it say?'

Brandish sighed. 'It said that anyone who takes a single piece of Huxley's treasure has three days before . . .'

'Before what?' Riz jumped in.

Brandish's eyes bored into hers. 'Before he comes to take it back.' He hauled himself out of his chair. 'It was as if Huxley himself had guided Podge's hand as he scratched it into the stone.'

In a hoarse whisper, like the sound of a sword being dragged across a wooden deck, Brandish closed his eyes and began to speak:

'Arisen from a watery grave,

a ghost ship you behold.

Beware the curse that falls upon

the fools who seek my gold.

The first day brings a salty sea,

the next a terrible grip,

the third will make you rue the day

you laid eyes on my ship.'

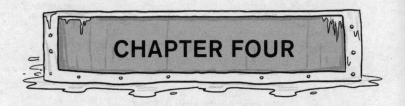

CHAPTER FOUR

'What a load of old nonsense! All the fish has pickled his brain!' Drew pulled the door of the Red Herring Fish Emporium shut behind them and checked his watch. 'That was such a waste of time.'

Olly looked doubtful as they set off down the main street of Snoops Bay, leaving the odour of fish behind them. 'I'm not so sure,' he muttered. 'Brandish seems to really believe it . . .'

'He's a washed-up old sea dog.' Drew laughed. 'He probably believes it's good luck for a bird to poo on you!'

'Isn't it?' asked Anton, looking disappointed.

As they headed back to collect their bikes from their hiding place in Snoops Bay park, Riz tried to shake the ominous feeling that had washed over her in Brandish's flat. Try as she might to laugh along with Drew about the so-called curse, a nervous feeling was gnawing at her insides, and the words of the poem echoed in her head.

'What if it's true?' Riz murmured. 'What if we're cursed?'

Drew looked at her as if she'd grown a second head. 'Riz, you surely don't believe that nonsense, do you?'

'Of course not!' She laughed half-heartedly. 'Well, actually . . .' she added. 'Maybe.'

'I do,' piped up Anton. 'I believe it all.'

'Yeah,' giggled Drew. 'But you believed me when I told you eating raw onions would make you grow faster!'

'Wait, is that not true?' Anton yelled indignantly.

The friends left the town behind them and crossed into Snoops Bay park. The sun had started to dip, grazing the tips of the oak trees that loomed over them. A chill wind was now bustling through the leaves, sending gentle whispers above their heads.

Olly was deep in thought. 'I'll do some research on this,' he said finally. 'Maybe the *Snoops Bay Sniffer* has some archive material on the *Captain's Revenge*.'

'How would they?' asked Drew. 'The ship's been buried at Bony Beach for three hundred years. Nobody even knew it was there!'

'What do you think the treasure is?' asked Anton. 'A big chest full of gold? Diamonds? Rubies? Gift vouchers?'

'It must have been quite something if Huxley spent two years looking for it,' said Olly.

'And if he put a curse on whoever found it,' Riz added.

Olly's face suddenly brightened. 'Wait a minute. Brandish said the curse would fall on whoever took the treasure from the ship. We haven't taken anything!'

Riz stopped in her tracks. 'You're right!' She beamed.

'We're in the clear!' squealed Anton, giving Olly a hard high-five and wincing as it stung his palm.

'We were always in the clear,' Drew muttered, aiming a kick at Anton's backside. 'C'mon, let's get our bikes.'

The four of them continued through the park, in higher spirits than before.

'Either way, let's keep this between us,' Riz added. Olly, Drew and Anton nodded in agreement. Cursed or not, that old ship was creepy, and the sooner it disappeared back under the sand, the better.

At last they reached their hiding place – an enormous bush that bent forward under its own weight, creating a curtain of foliage that shielded the bikes from prying eyes and fingers. As they dragged them out and dusted some stray pine needles from their saddles, they suddenly heard twigs snapping on the path behind them. All four of them whipped around.

'What was that?' Anton gasped as they stood rooted to the spot.

Riz shushed him and glanced at Olly and Drew, who were also standing frozen in fright. 'Did you hear that?'

They all nodded rapidly, their eyes like saucers. Riz peered down the path, which seemed empty. The trees leant in from either side, and a trail yawned out in front of them in the burnt orange light of the setting sun. But it was silent.

There was another sound of a twig snapping, followed by a loud rustle.

'Who's there?' yelled Riz, her voice wavering.

More rustling of leaves, and then the bush immediately to the group's left exploded into life. It sprouted a pair of legs and arms, then rugby-tackled Riz to the ground before straddling her with a triumphant guffaw.

'Well, *hello*!' trilled the bush. 'Have you a moment for *GossWorld*?'

Riz bucked wildly, gasping for air. 'Get off me!' she huffed. 'What are you playing at?'

Over her shoulder came the sound of Olly's voice. 'Tiara, you frightened us half to death!'

Olly hauled Riz upright. She stumbled to her feet and stared furiously into the face of the bush.

Upon closer inspection, it wasn't a bush at all. A girl's face had appeared from within the foliage, daubed with smears of green and brown paint, and two smug brown eyes peered out from under a green helmet.

'Tiara Turbot!' growled Riz. 'I should have known.'

A victorious grin was plastered across Tiara's face. 'Rizandra Sekhon. How lovely to see you!' She smirked. 'I'm on the hunt for some stories for the latest issue of *GossWorld*. I hope you'll be picking up a copy?'

'Who would read that rag?' Olly interrupted, his face flushed. 'You only started making that magazine because I created *Unearthed*! You don't even care about finding real stories. All you do is lie and pretend it's journalism!'

Tiara wrinkled her nose at him, as if she'd caught a whiff of something unpleasant. In fairness, the group had just spent quite some time in a fishmonger's.

'*GossWorld* is not a *rag*, mud boy!' she snapped. 'We're the number-one showbiz and celebrity gossip magazine in town!'

'Gossip?' Olly spluttered. 'That's not journalism!'

'Tell that to the mayor!' shot back Tiara. 'He reads it every month!'

'It helps that he's your dad!' Olly said loudly.

Riz looked Tiara up and down in bewilderment. 'Why are you dressed like a bush?'

Tiara's arms and legs were covered in a tangled mess of leaves and twigs, and it looked as though she'd even glued some bark to her costume. She pulled out a thick pink notepad, along with a sickly green pen that she twirled smugly in Riz's face.

'*The Hill twins step out on a summer evening with local troublemaker Riz Sekhon, and renowned mud nerd, Olly Rudd!*' she declared. She suddenly plucked an enormous camera from underneath her costume and shoved it in their faces. 'Say cheese!' she commanded. There was a blinding flash of light and a loud *snap*.

'Ow!' Riz flung her arm over her face. 'Watch where you're pointing that!'

Tiara shoved past her, already stowing the camera away. She marched up to Drew and poised her pen over her notebook. 'Drew, is there any truth in the rumour that you and your brother are actually the same person in different-coloured wigs?' she demanded.

'Obviously not,' piped up Anton. 'I'm standing right here!'

Tiara scribbled furiously. *Hill would neither confirm nor deny the rumour.*

'I just told you it's not true!' repeated Anton.

Tiara held up an imperious finger in front of Anton, signalling for him to be quiet. 'What about your schoolwork? A very reliable source told me you failed a spelling test two weeks ago and came bottom of the class!'

Drew turned a bright shade of pink and looked at the ground. Anton growled and stepped between Tiara and his brother. He was a good deal shorter than her, but glared up at her fiercely.

'That's none of your business, Tiara!' he told her. 'Leave us alone!'

'This is the sort of juicy gossip my readers love!' Tiara replied. 'Now get out of my face, unless you want me to write an exclusive story about how you get all your clothes from the second-hand shop!'

'So what?' Anton's hands were balled into fists. Drew began to tug him backwards.

'How do you know all this, Tiara?' Riz demanded. 'Have you been spying on us?'

Tiara tittered. 'Of course I have! That's what every good journalist does.'

'No, they don't!' yelled Olly.

'I've had you four under surveillance for weeks.' Tiara ignored him and started ticking off an imaginary list. 'The winner's enclosure at the racecourse. Do you remember the funny-shaped little pony that followed you around that day?'

'That was you?' gasped Anton.

'The summer barbeque in the square,' Tiara continued. 'There was a huge roast hog that screamed when my daddy tried to put it on the spit?'

'That was you too?' Drew choked.

'And the library fundraiser in this very park. I was an enormous beanbag in the clearing, and Olly sat on me!'

'I did think that was a particularly lumpy beanbag,' muttered Olly.

'They were all me in disguise!' cackled Tiara. 'I must have spent nearly the entire *GossWorld* budget in Burpy Gumby's Fancy Dress Shop.' With a flourish, she produced the receipt, which curled down past her knees.

BURPY GUMBY'S FANCY DRESS SHOP RECEIPT

'All paid for by Daddy, of course.' She smiled at the Hill brothers. 'When your daddy is the mayor, money's not a problem.' Then she bundled her costume together and stuffed her notepad back under the foliage. 'See you later, losers!' she sneered. 'Don't forget to pick up your copy of *GossWorld* tomorrow!'

The four friends stared open-mouthed as Tiara Turbot marched back down the path, merging with the greenery once more.

CHAPTER FIVE

The next morning, the building that housed the Snoops Bay public swimming pool was packed. A thick blue covering had been hauled over the pool itself, and the chatter of hundreds of residents bounced off the high vaulted ceiling, making the huge windows rattle. The crowd sat before a raised platform in front of the pool, eagerly awaiting the arrival of the mayor.

Riz, Olly, Drew and Anton squeezed their way past two fierce-looking old ladies (security guard caps perched atop their perms) and found themselves seats in the viewing area overlooking the platform and pool. An enormous advertisement had been unfurled, and its gaudy red-and-green text hurt to look at.

Riz turned to Olly. 'Do you ever think about how strange this town is?' she muttered.

'Not a chance,' he told her. 'I'm hoping to get a sit-down interview with Keith and Judith before they swim off, as an exclusive for *Unearthed*!'

'How does an eel sit down?' she wondered aloud.

Every Easter, the town of Snoops Bay went eel crazy. Over the long weekend, the harbour and town centre were overrun with eel enthusiasts, tourists, residents who should know better, and local celebrities looking to get their faces on the front page of the *Snoops Bay Sniffer*. They never did, though. The front page was always reserved for a photo of the star attraction: Keith and Judith the sea eels, pictured training for their annual five-thousand-mile trip.

When the clock struck noon on the third day of the Festiv-Eel, Snoops Bay harbour was packed with people waving flags, setting off fireworks and licking eel-shaped ice lollies while they tried to catch a glimpse of Keith and Judith swimming by. In Riz's opinion, the entire festival was extremely stupid.

'How long do eels live for?' she'd once asked her dad as they milled around the harbour, waiting for Mayor Turbot to fire the starting water pistol to send Keith and Judith on their way. He had shushed her quickly. 'As long as it takes for tourists to pull out their wallets and spend some cash!'

To the side of the platform was a buffet table, groaning under the weight of fish and other seafood provided by Captain Jasper Brandish of the Red Herring Fish Emporium. A creamy chowder bubbled merrily on the table, accompanied by every shape and size of fish and crustacean plucked from the ocean. Brandish winked at the group of friends as he spooned mountains of

steaming fish onto paper plates. Kourtney the blobfish sat in her bowl, eyeing the seafood nervously.

Beside Brandish's buffet stood an iced-tea stall manned by Tiara Turbot in full chef's regalia, including white hat and glued-on pencil moustache. She stuck her tongue out at the four of them.

There was a sudden smattering of applause and Mayor Turbot bounded onto the platform. Despite having been mayor of Snoops Bay for almost thirty years, he never seemed to be able to locate an iron. His clothes were perpetually crumpled, and he was forever dabbing sweat from his brow and the back of his neck. Whenever he became excited, which was often, his wig would wobble like a tower of hairy jelly, and his skin was permanently tinged with a faint orange glow – the type of tan that (according to Olly's mum) he could only have achieved via a trip to Tina's Tanning Salon. He also had the irritating habit of constantly perching his glasses on the end of his nose before whipping them off and gesticulating wildly to make a point. He would then clean them, place them back on his nose, and the whole cycle would begin again.

'Good morning, friends and neighbours!' declared the mayor. A hush fell across the room. 'Welcome, one and all,' he boomed, 'to the first day of Snoops Bay's hundredth annual Festiv-Eel!'

The crowd broke into an eager round of applause, and Tiara Turbot threw her chef's hat in the air triumphantly.

'Once again,' the mayor continued, 'the time has come for us to say our goodbyes, for now, to Keith and Judith, as they begin their journey to the Sargasso Sea.

These special eels have been training intensely for the last three months to get ready for this great journey that they've made so many times before. And we, as a town, are ready to welcome those who have travelled from far and wide to open their wallets ... I mean, their hearts, and bid them a fond farewell.' He threw a sideways glance at his daughter, who gave him a pleading shake of the head. 'Or should that be a fond *farew-eel*?'

No one laughed. Tiara shot him a sour look.

'Moving on,' he said quickly, 'our first event of the Festiv-Eel is about to get underway. Today, we open the festival with the much-anticipated Pufferfish Puff-Off to find the puffiest puffer in Snoops Bay. Tomorrow, the doors of Snoops Bay aquarium will be thrown open for an access-all-areas tour with eel-trainer extraordinaire, Squid O'Malley.'

The crowd bobbed their heads in excitement.

'And on our third and final day, we'll bid Keith and Judith farewell with our Sargasso Sea send-off at the harbour. So, without further ado ...' The mayor's hands shot into the air. 'Will you please put your fins and flippers together for ... the pufferfish!'

'The Pufferfish Puff-Off!' squealed Anton, hardly able

to contain his excitement. Drew rolled his eyes.

The crammed poolside burst into applause. 'That's right!' The mayor beamed. 'Please make way for the Puffing Pool!'

A rusty squeaking of wheels sounded, and a long shallow paddling pool was pulled out in front of the platform by a team of volunteers wearing Festiv-Eel T-shirts. A panel of judges took their positions beside the paddling pool, pencils poised above their clipboards. A stern-looking lady with the nametag HEAD JUDGE

dipped a thermometer into the water and inspected it. She looked up and gave a sharp nod to the mayor.

'Bring out the puffers!' bellowed the mayor.

Riz, Olly, Drew and Anton watched from their seats as a procession of people made their way to the paddling pool and carefully plopped their pufferfish into the water. Each fish wore a tiny red collar attached to a leash, which their owner held in their fist.

'I have ten quid on number four,' Riz heard Tiara Turbot say from her iced-tea stand. 'C'MON, BUBBLES!' she roared over the chatter of the crowd.

The pufferfish were now being led around the paddling pool by their owners.

'All right, contestants!' came Mayor Turbot's voice. 'On your marks . . . get set . . .'

Silence fell over the pool. 'PUFF!' he shouted.

The owners by the side of the paddling pool gave an encouraging tug on their leashes, and every pufferfish ballooned to ten times its original size. The watching crowd roared in approval as the eyes of each fish bulged outwards.

'Now that's some impressive puffery! But which pufferfish is the biggest?' Mayor Turbot commentated as the panel of judges scribbled furiously. Tiara Turbot had now whipped off her chef's costume and was eagerly snapping photos for *GossWorld*.

'Get your one to puff towards the camera!' she ordered a bewildered owner.

'Tiara Turbot really grates my gills,' grumbled Olly, watching her with narrowed eyes.

Suddenly, there came a *pop* from the far end of the paddling pool.

'Oh dear!' declared Mayor Turbot. 'We've got a popper! There goes Bubbles' chance.' Tiara gave a wail of defeat.

'Right, folks, it looks like the judges have chosen a winner. Give it up for Jiggles and his owner Sue!' Mayor Turbot smiled and started pinning a first-place rosette on the inflated pufferfish. There was another loud *pop*. 'Oops, the pin slipped!' Mayor Turbot winced, and quickly ushered the bereft-looking owner away.

Moments later, a clatter sounded behind the audience, and everyone whipped round in fright. The door at the rear of the building had burst open and a woman was striding purposefully towards Mayor Turbot. She wore a white linen shirt tucked under a leather waistcoat with brown trousers and high leather boots, which hammered on the tiles, sending quivers through Tiara's enormous bowl of iced tea.

The woman bounded onto the platform with a single leap, and as she whirled round to face the audience, her green eyes narrowed under the brim of her battered fedora hat.

She raised her right arm, then brought it crashing down, and a snake-like shape curled over her head. A crack as loud as a gunshot echoed through the room. She then rolled the long brown whip round her arm and hung it nonchalantly from her shoulder.

Mayor Turbot, who had only just dodged the whip, looked irritated by the interruption. 'Ah, Squid,' he said through clenched teeth. 'Thank you for joining us.' He bowed to the woman standing before him, then addressed the crowd. 'Most of you will already know our guest. However, for those who don't, may I introduce Squid O'Malley, the manager of the Snoops Bay aquarium and part-time eel-trainer to the stars, and Keith and Judith's proud owner!'

Squid O'Malley gave a grunt and tipped the brim of her hat. 'Glad to be here,' she growled, in a way that suggested she was not at all glad to be there.

'How's training been going?' asked Mayor Turbot meekly. 'Are Keith and Judith well?'

Squid gave a curt nod. 'They're in peak condition. I took them out for a quick fifteen-mile swim around the bay this morning. They're in the finest shape they've ever been in. Keith pulled a muscle on the final mile, but a quick deep-tissue massage sorted it right out.'

'Well, that's excellent!' The mayor clapped. 'Would you care to take a seat? We've just selected the winner of the Puff-Off.'

Squid cut across Mayor Turbot faster than the crack of her whip. 'I'm afraid I'm not here to discuss childish competitions, mayor. I've brought disturbing news.'

The building filled with a deathly silence, and the colour (or at least some of it) drained from the mayor's face.

'Oh! What is it . . . ?' he asked, as if he didn't really want to know the answer.

Squid placed her hands on her hips, her face grim, and surveyed the crowd before her suspiciously. 'On our swim around the bay this morning, we took a quick detour so that Judith could use the bathroom.'

The mayor looked confused. 'The bathroom?'

'We swam into shore by Bony Beach,' continued Squid. Her eyes narrowed as she scanned the faces of the townspeople and tourists in front of her.

The four friends fidgeted nervously.

'I'm sorry to report that someone has been digging there,' said Squid. 'And they've discovered something . . . *terrible*.'

'Something terrible? On Bony Beach?' The mayor

looked anxiously around the room.

'A ship!' barked Squid, causing everyone present to jump in fright. She drew herself up to her full, considerable height and declared, 'Tis the wreck of the *Captain's Revenge*! It was last seen three hundred years ago, when Captain Horatio Huxley drowned with it, leaving behind a fateful curse!'

CHAPTER SIX

There was a long pause as the townsfolk processed what Squid had announced. She plucked her hat from her head and strode over to the iced-tea table.

'Iced tea?' offered Tiara weakly.

'Haven't you got anything stronger?' snapped Squid.

Mayor Turbot giggled nervously as he struggled to mop up the waterfall of sweat that was now cascading down his brow. He gestured through clenched teeth for the volunteers to drag away the paddling pool, now full of deflated pufferfish, while Squid begrudgingly poured herself an iced tea.

'Oh, come now, Ms O'Malley.' The mayor turned to Squid. 'You can't expect us to believe all that nonsense about Huxley's curse.'

'It's not nonsense!' came a voice from the buffet table.

The residents of Snoops Bay turned and watched as Brandish limped up to the platform and waggled a ladle at the mayor. Tiara's camera bulb flashed again.

'This is the best gossip I've ever heard!' she squeaked to no one in particular.

'The curse is real, Mayor Turbot,' Brandish stated. 'I truly wish it wasn't, but every fisherman and sailor in Snoops Bay knows the fate of the unfortunate soul who messes around with that ship!'

'Doom!' bellowed Squid, squashing her untouched paper cup and creating an explosion of iced tea.

'Doom!' agreed Brandish.

'Doooooom!' echoed more voices from the crowd. A buzz of nervous murmurs rose in volume until Squid cracked her whip hard on the platform.

Mayor Turbot fidgeted with his hands nervously. 'But what sort of doom . . . ?'

'DOOM!' piped up Tiara Turbot.

'SHUT IT!' yelled the mayor. Then he turned to Brandish and jabbed a stubby finger in his direction. 'What sort of doom are you babbling on about, Brandish?'

Brandish shrugged. 'That's all I know, mayor.' He turned to face the crowd, his eyes falling on Riz,

Olly, Drew and Anton, and recited the curse. Then he continued, 'Mayor Turbot, you must cancel the Festiv-Eel.'

Shouts of despair rang out through the room.

'Impossible!'

'He's off his head!'

'I've got two hundred Keith and Judith commemorative plates in my boot. What am I going to do with them?'

'Please, everyone! We will not be cancelling the Festiv-Eel!' Mayor Turbot shouted above the din. He threw a withering look at Brandish, who was shaking his head silently. 'The weekend will proceed as planned!' continued the mayor. 'Unless of course –' he turned back to Squid, his eyebrows raised innocently – 'the world-famous eel-tamer, Squid O'Malley, is *frightened* of a fisherman's tale about treasure and curses?'

Squid stiffened, curling her whip threateningly round her feet. 'Squid O'Malley and her eels are frightened of nothing – living or dead! It's the curse that should fear us!'

A smug grin spread across the mayor's face. 'Well, then,' he said, his voice dripping with honey. 'We shall proceed!' Turning back to the crowd, he raised his hands in victory. 'Let us forget all this nonsense about curses and focus on the real reason we're here today. I propose a toast!' shouted Mayor Turbot. The audience eagerly rushed for refills of iced tea. Tiara passed her dad an overflowing cup and he raised it to the ceiling. 'A toast to Keith and Judith!'

Olly, Drew and Anton had joined in the cheering, pushing through the throng to get teas. Riz rolled her eyes. She felt a hand come down on her shoulder and turned to find a worried-looking Brandish.

'We must make sure no one goes near that ship,' he rasped. 'If a single piece of that treasure is taken, in three days we'll all be—'

'Oh, relax, Brandish!' Drew reappeared and butted in. 'It's all a load of old—'

But he never finished his sentence as a blood-curdling shriek stabbed through the room.

Mayor Turbot was doubled over on the platform, coughing and spluttering madly. 'I think I'm going to be sick!' He choked.

Another scream rang from the side of the platform. Tiara had spat her iced tea all over a shocked-looking gentleman. 'Eurghhh,' she yelled, her face turning bright red.

All over the room, people were gagging and retching, spraying their neighbours with Tiara's iced tea. Anton was standing with his own paper cup raised to his mouth, ready to throw it down his gullet.

A second later, a *crack* split the air, and Anton's cup exploded in a shower of paper and liquid. Squid yanked back her whip and pointed accusingly at the bowl of iced tea.

'Sabotage!' she bellowed.

Mayor Turbot had fallen to his knees, his eyes pink and

stinging with tears. 'TIARA!' he roared over the sound of spluttering. 'WHAT ON EARTH IS IN THE TEA?'

'PEACH AND POMEGRANATE!' she shrieked back, surveying the scene before her in horror.

Squid snatched a cup from the table and sipped it carefully. She grimaced and spat.

'Seawater!' she declared. 'The tea has been laced with it!'

Chaos reigned throughout the building. Brandish and Mayor Turbot shouted and pointed fingers in each other's faces, while townsfolk and tourists spluttered and yelled in disbelief. One of the Festiv-Eel volunteers was even performing a Heimlich manoeuvre on Tiara.

'"The first day brings a salty sea"!' gasped Anton. His eyes were wide in fear as he looked at his friends. 'The curse has begun!'

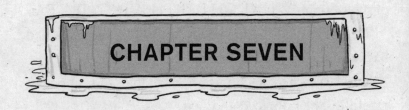

CHAPTER SEVEN

'I still don't see how this is our fault,' insisted Drew, crossing his arms stubbornly.

Anton pinched the bridge of his nose in frustration and helped himself to another of Olly's mum's gingerbread men. 'What part of setting off a three-hundred-year-old curse do you not understand, Drew?'

The Pufferfish Puff-Off event had ended in pandemonium, with the attendees dashing off to buy as much mouthwash as they could find in Snoops Bay. A crestfallen Mayor Turbot had addressed the crowd once he'd reattached his wig.

'We've been the victims of a prank!' he announced to the crowd. 'Someone wants to sabotage the Festiv-Eel and undo all the money we're going to make—' At that point, Tiara cleared her voice loudly. 'I mean,' he corrected himself quickly, 'undo all the hard work that Keith and Judith have done!'

'Let's burn the ship!' a voice from the back rang out.

Mayor Turbot looked horrified. 'Bony Beach will be off limits until the Festiv-Eel is over,' he told the crowd. 'No one goes near that ship this weekend, by order of the mayor! After that, we'll turn it into a sightseeing spot.'

The audience murmured their reluctant agreement.

'You're playing a dangerous game with an evil spirit!' Brandish warned the mayor before grabbing Kourtney's fishbowl and securing it to a little skateboard attached to his belt with a leash. 'Tomorrow,' he yelled over his shoulder, 'the curse will return!'

Riz, Olly, Drew and Anton sped back to Olly's house and slammed the door to his bedroom (pausing for snacks on the way through the kitchen). They now sat cross-legged on his bedroom floor and pondered what on earth had just happened.

'We uncovered the ship, and now Captain Horatio Huxley is coming to take his revenge!' shrilled Anton, spraying gingerbread crumbs from his mouth. He was still wearing an enormous Festiv-Eel novelty hat.

'You're beginning to sound like Brandish!' Drew snorted. 'It's a load of old nonsense!' He turned to Riz pleadingly. 'It's nonsense, right?'

'I mean, there was seawater in the tea, Drew ...' she said. 'It's spooky!'

'Someone was obviously just having a laugh,' Drew said with a wave of his hand.

'You're beginning to sound like Turbot!' snapped Anton, breaking the head off a gingerbread man with more force than was required.

Olly was silent, seemingly lost in thought as he nibbled the backside of his gingerbread man. Drew prodded him with his toe. 'Olly, you're a journalist. What do you think?'

Olly frowned hard. 'Well ...' he began slowly. 'Any good journalist knows that information is only as good as its source.'

'Exactly!' crowed Drew. 'And our only source is a pickled old sea captain who keeps a blobfish in a bowl and talks to it!'

'Not quite,' Olly contradicted, tucking the leg of a gingerbread man behind his ear like a pencil. 'In fact –' he continued, frowning harder – 'we have two separate sources here: Captain Jasper Brandish and Squid O'Malley. She believes in the curse too.'

'Squid is awesome!' piped up Anton. 'She saved my life!'

'Let's not be overdramatic, Anton,' Riz told him.

Olly sprang to his feet and began to pace up and down his bedroom like he always did when he was chewing over a story. 'That being said,' he went on, 'the likelihood of there being an actual curse on the town seems extremely slim.'

'Non-existent!' said Drew, nodding in agreement.

'That being said,' Olly continued, 'someone did lace the iced tea with seawater, which is proof that the curse is in motion.'

'Exactly!' agreed Anton.

'*That* being said,' Olly frowned harder, 'the curse is only meant to come into effect if something is *taken* from the ship. And we didn't take anything!' He stopped pacing for a moment. 'That being said . . .'

'IT'S ALL BEEN SAID!' exploded Riz. 'Just tell us what you think and be done with it!'

Olly didn't reply. His face had dropped as if he'd suddenly realized he'd left a sandwich in the bottom of his schoolbag for a year. He slowly turned towards his pals, and a shiver of dread washed over the three of them.

'Olly . . .' Riz prompted. 'What is it?'

His voice was barely more than a whisper. 'We *did* take something,' he rasped. 'We took samples from around the ship!'

Drew gave a short laugh, but it was tinged with nerves. 'What, a few jars of muck and seaweed? That's not treasure, Olly.'

Olly dived over to his mud shelf and began sweeping jars left and right, muttering as he read each label. 'Stinking Fairy, Emu Dung, Cave Juice . . .'

'Careful of the carpet!' Riz winced.

'Found it!' Olly yelled. He carefully placed his largest jar on the rug as if he was handling radioactive waste. 'This is the muck from under the *Captain's Revenge*.'

The four friends sat and stared at the jar of brown goo in silence.

'Drew's right, Olly,' Riz told him. 'It doesn't look like treasure to me.'

Olly twisted the lid off the jar with grim determination, and a billowing cloud of muck particles rose into the sunlight streaming through the windows. He pulled the half-eaten gingerbread man from behind his ear and stuck it into the jar, prodding around in the gloop.

'I would've eaten that!' grumbled Anton.

Within the muck, Olly could see various lumps and shapes, and he looked around for an implement to fish them out. 'Anyone got a spoon?'

'Oh, give it here,' snapped Drew, yanking the novelty hat from Anton's head and pouring the entire contents of the jar into it.

'DREW!' yelled Anton. 'THAT'S MY HAT!'

Drew carefully plucked the lumps from the mud and wiped them down.

Olly held the first item up to the light. 'One set of false teeth, caked with mud.' Riz made a note. He held up the next. 'One crab leg, without its owner.' Riz noted the crab leg, and Olly went on. A few strands of seaweed, a couple of shells, and then the hat was empty.

'See, no treasure here!' said Drew finally. 'We're safe.'

'Wait!' Riz had spotted something glimmering in the oozy muck. She reached in, wincing at the feel of the cold muck, and pulled it out.

The four of them stared in horrified silence at what Riz was now holding between her fingers.

'It's gold!' gasped Olly in disbelief. 'A gold coin, no less!'

'Show me that!' Drew reached over and snatched the coin from Riz's grasp. He inspected it carefully, then looked up at the group. A gulp throbbed in his throat. 'We need to put this back right away.'

CHAPTER EIGHT

The friends had never cycled faster in their lives. The normal way to Bony Beach had been closed with immediate effect by order of Mayor Turbot, and a chain-link fence had been erected to keep out curious tourists, so they'd had to re-route.

They pedalled out of Snoops Bay and soon joined the rough bicycle track that led into the forest, past the academy that had once been run by Madame Strang, and towards Bony Beach.

'This is all your fault!' Riz yelled at Olly, puffing madly as they flew through the trees. She eyed each bush nervously as if Captain Huxley was about to spring out and swipe at them with his cutlass.

'My fault?' gasped Olly indignantly. 'This is all Drew's fault! If he'd believed in the curse sooner, then—'

'*My fault?*' shouted Drew from his bike. 'This is all Riz's fault! If Riz hadn't started digging in that spot—'

'MY FAULT?' Riz yelled back at him. 'It was Olly's idea to go to Bony Beach in the first place!'

'Does anyone think it was *my* fault?' asked Anton from his perch behind Drew's saddle.

They all fell silent. Strangely, Anton seemed annoyed to have been left out.

'It's all under control,' Olly said calmly. 'We'll just pop back to the ship, leave the coin where we found it—'

'*Pop back?*' yelled Riz. 'There could be a whole army of zombie pirates waiting for us!'

'Listen to yourselves!' butted in Drew. 'Zombie pirates, curses! This is all one big prank, I guarantee it.'

'ANTON!' Riz shouted back. 'Will you please give Drew a poke in the ribs?'

'With pleasure!' Anton yelled, and a moment later Drew yelped in pain.

The track beneath the bikes slowly began to fade under the grey sand of the dunes, and they decided to continue their journey on foot. They stowed their bikes under a clump of marram grass (making sure none of the surrounding plants were Tiara Turbot in disguise) and tramped down the dunes towards the beach.

As they finally climbed down the last steep incline, Olly made a strangled noise. 'Stop!' He threw his arms out to either side, bringing them all skidding to a halt.

'What?' Riz gulped.

Olly pointed a trembling finger down to the beach, his voice faltering in fear. 'We may have a problem,' he gasped.

Riz straightened up and squinted at the shoreline. 'Uh-oh.'

Like a monstrous dinosaur rising from its grave, the wreck of the *Captain's Revenge* was almost completely unearthed, and now stood upright on the beach. Its enormous masts towered towards the sky, a few ragged scraps of rotting sail still clinging to them. A gang of seagulls was circling the broken bucket that had once been the crow's nest, and for a moment it seemed like the ship would turn towards the ocean and set sail again. Only the jagged hole punched deep into the hull hinted that it was a broken, dead ship.

A ghost ship, thought Olly with a shiver.

'It's the right way up,' said Anton in barely more than

a whisper. His hand suddenly searched for his brother's. Drew took it and gave it a little squeeze.

'C'mon,' Drew said, beginning to climb down the dunes towards the ship. 'Let's check it out.'

'Are you crazy?' squeaked Olly. 'It's risen from the dead and now it's waiting for us!'

'There's got to be an explanation,' Drew said firmly. 'And we're not going to be able to work it out if we're sitting here scared!'

'What about Captain Huxley?' Anton trembled. 'What about the curse?'

Drew sighed, his hands resting on his hips. 'Well, the only way to break the curse is to return what we took from the ship, so let's get moving!'

Riz, Olly and Anton stood in silence, contemplating their options. 'I think Drew may have a point.' Riz shrugged.

Olly sighed and pulled a wad of paper towel from his pocket. He unwrapped it, revealing the little gold coin tucked inside. He looked at the coin, then down to the dark shape of the *Captain's Revenge*, then back again. 'Okay,' he said finally, tucking the coin back into his jeans. 'Let's go.'

Anton's knees knocked together in fright. 'I'm scared!'

'You're a Hill!' Drew told him with a grin. 'Hills aren't scared of dusty old pirate zombies!'

'I think you'll find we most certainly are!' Anton replied, but he allowed himself to be led down the dunes towards the hulking mass of the ship. 'If Captain Huxley tries any funny business, I'm out of here!' he told Riz solemnly. She tried to give him a brave smile but it faltered on her lips.

They eventually reached level ground and stood directly under the ship. Up close, the damage was more obvious – jagged holes in the wood leered at them like huge jaws, and a damp wind whistled around the hull. The breeze sent the ragged sails dancing high above their heads with a mournful sigh.

'How on earth did it get out of the sand?' Riz wondered aloud.

Olly was studying the ground carefully. 'Look at this.' He beckoned Riz over. 'Someone's been here.'

Riz leant over his shoulder – he was right. A faint set of footprints were set into the wet sand, accompanied by two wheel-tracks. They snaked from the dunes, round the ship, and then disappeared into the sea.

'Someone on foot,' Olly said. 'And I guess two on bikes. Three people have been here!'

'Come and look at this!' Anton called them over.

Riz and Olly left the footprints behind and followed the sound of his voice around the other side of the shipwreck. Two wide tyre-tracks emerged from the sea, leading directly to the ship and then back into the water. They gazed at the marks, stupefied.

'Maybe it's some sort of machinery?' Olly guessed.

'That can travel underwater?' said Riz. 'It came from the sea!'

'A zombie tractor!' cried Anton.

Olly pulled a crumpled sheaf of notes from his rucksack. 'What time is it?' he barked to Drew, who'd appeared around the side of the ship.

Drew checked his watch. 'Half past four,' he said. 'Why?'

Olly studied a long set of figures on the paper in front of him and narrowed his eyes. 'According to this,' he said eventually, 'we're nearly at high tide. And low tide today was . . . three hours ago.'

'So?' said Drew.

Olly stuffed his notes back into his bag. 'So whoever

left these tyre tracks didn't want anyone to follow them. They must have come here at low tide, driven right beside the water's edge, done what they needed to do with the ship, then driven back down the water's edge and home again. Then when the sea came back in, the tracks were partly washed away. If we'd come a few hours later, they'd have gone completely!'

There was a long pause.

'Olly, you're a great journalist,' said Riz finally. 'And not a bad detective too! Has anyone ever told you that?'

Olly tried to avoid looking smug, but he didn't entirely succeed.

'Maybe it was some sort of crane,' Drew suggested, pointing at the size of the tracks. 'To lift the ship upright.'

'Maybe . . .' Olly screwed up his eyes and looked at the crow's nest. 'Whatever or whoever it was, they covered their tracks . . . literally.'

'It could have been someone looking for the treasure?' said Riz suddenly.

'Could be,' Olly said, frowning hard. 'Or a nosy parker snooping around . . .'

They all simultaneously let out a groan that was snatched up and away by the wind.

'Tiara Turbot.' Olly grimaced. 'She's just the type who'd want the entire town to be cursed. She'd love the drama!'

Another whip of wind encircled them, and they all shivered.

'Let's get this over with,' Riz said quickly.

'I agree,' said Olly, throwing an impatient glance at Drew, who was busy trying to scratch some of the seaweed off the underbelly of the *Captain's Revenge*. 'Drew! Let's go!'

'I've never seen a real shipwreck before!' protested Drew. 'Do you think we'll find any swords inside?'

'The only sword we're going to find is the one Captain Horatio Huxley sticks in us if we don't *hurry up*!' snapped Anton. 'Just toss the coin into that hole and let's get out of here!'

They plodded around the side of the ship and peered through the crater in the hull. It was pitch black, the darkness stretching deep into the belly of the *Captain's Revenge*. Somewhere inside, a gust was rattling the ship's skeleton, and the thick wooden planks moaned and creaked in protest. Olly sniffed the wind. There was a dank whiff of rotting wood and bird droppings.

'Can you see anything?' whispered Anton, craning his neck to try to see inside.

Drew shook his head. 'It looks empty.'

'Well, throw in the coin!' urged Anton. 'C'mon, Olly. Let's get out of here!'

Olly unwrapped the coin and held it up thoughtfully. He cleared his throat over the wind. 'Ahem. Hello, Captain Huxley!' he called into the ship.

'Don't talk to him!' squealed Anton in horror. 'Just throw it!'

Olly shushed him. 'Hello, Captain Huxley,' he called again. 'And ... erm ... top of the morning to you!'

'That's what leprechauns say, not pirates!' hissed Riz.

'We wanted to let you know,' continued Olly, 'that we're very sorry for taking one of your coins. We didn't mean to. Although, if you wreak bloody revenge upon any of us, the *guiltiest* culprit is probably Drew.'

'Olly!' Drew looked to Riz and Anton, who were nodding their heads in enthusiastic agreement. Above them, the rags of the sail were whipping angrily in the wind.

'Anyway,' Olly went on. 'We're very sorry if we've caused you any upset or worry. Please don't arise from your watery grave and get us in our sleep. Deal?'

Silence.

Riz shrugged. 'Well, go on, then. Throw it!'

Olly drew his hand back and sent the coin sailing into the darkness inside the *Captain's Revenge*. There was a loud *clink* as it landed and rolled along the floor followed by silence. They all let out a collective sigh of relief.

'Well, that settles it,' said Anton, giving a small salute. 'Now can we please—'

A tiny patch of white caught Riz's eye. 'What's that?' She pointed.

'What's what?' squeaked Anton.

'There's something nestled in the wood.' Riz took a closer look. A tiny wedge of parchment was sticking out of a hole in the hull, wrapped up and jammed in tight. 'Someone's left a piece of paper behind.' She dug her fingernails deep into the hole, tugging hard to dislodge the parchment.

She finally managed to pluck out a yellowed and stained strip of paper, then shook some salty droplets off it and carefully unrolled it. It was sopping wet, stained by ink that had merged into a fat blue splotch across the paper. Riz squinted down at it, trying to make out the blobs of letters. When she finally deciphered the scrawl, she let out a high shriek and dropped the paper onto the ground.

'What's happened?' yelled Drew, diving past her and clawing the note from the sand.

'What does it say, Drew?' Olly grabbed Riz by the shoulders. 'Riz, are you okay?'

Drew was staring grimly at the fluttering scrap. Wordlessly, he passed it to Olly, who stared down at it in horror.

'Well?' demanded Anton in a wobbly voice.

Olly glanced at Riz, who was shivering all over, then at Drew, before his gaze finally landed on Anton.

He cleared his throat. 'It's a message ... from ... Captain Huxley!'

Anton looked as if he was about to faint. He grabbed the paper and ogled it, before dropping it with a strangled gasp.

CHAPTER NINE

'We have to get out of here!' Anton pleaded, grabbing Drew by the arm.

'Watch it!' Drew yelled, snatching the paper off the ground and dusting the sand from it. 'This is a clue!'

'A clue to what?' Anton demanded, hopping nervously from foot to foot and eyeing the scrap as if it were about to burst into flames. 'It's clearly Huxley warning us to get the hell out of here!'

'Anton's right,' said Riz, shooting a nervous look at Drew. 'Something's not right here. We should go.'

Drew opened his mouth to argue, but he stopped when he noticed something moving in the darkness inside the ship. Then came a sharp skittering that fell silent just as quickly as it had begun. It sounded like a shoe scraping across wood, or a pebble being kicked along a rotten floorboard.

Anton grabbed Riz's elbow in a tight squeeze. 'What was that?'

They stood before the ship, rooted to the sand.

'Time to leave,' said Olly quickly. He was gazing into the darkness, where shapes and shadows seemed to form in the gloom – grinning skeletons slowly crawling towards them, empty eye-sockets leering as they came ever closer.

Drew suddenly stepped towards the hole. 'Is there someone in there?' he said in a loud voice. 'Show yourselves!'

'DREW!' yelled Anton, looking as if he was about to be sick. 'Let's GO!'

Drew shushed him, leaning closer to the hole and listening hard.

'*Helloooo,*' he called into the darkness, his voice echoing back towards them from the depths of the ship. 'Anybody home?'

'This is ridiculous!' Anton turned to Riz and Olly, who were still standing rigid and uncertain. 'Let's get the bikes and head home. Then we can forget all about Huxley, his treasure, and the plague of bloodthirsty zombie pirates that could appear at any minute!'

'There may be a problem with that plan, Anton ...
Your brother has just climbed inside the ship,' Riz said.

Anton whirled back round to face the ship. Drew was
gone. He gaped for a second, then threw his arms up in
despair. 'Well, there we have it! The bloodthirsty zombie
pirates got him,' he announced. 'I tried to warn you all!'
He marched up to Olly and pointed an accusing finger
in his face. 'I tried to be the sensible one for once, but
would anyone listen? No! And now the three of us will
have to go to the police station and file a report that says
my brother's been snatched by pirates!'

Olly winced. 'There may be a problem with that plan,
Anton.' He pointed back towards the hole. 'Riz has just
climbed inside the ship too.'

Anton whipped his head round. Sure enough, Riz had
also disappeared. Anton's face turned the colour of a
burst strawberry. 'Well, that does it!' He choked in fury.
'If my brother and Riz are idiotic enough to climb inside
a haunted pirate ship, then I'm sure Captain Huxley will
be more than happy to have them!'

He began to march back up the beach in the
direction of the dunes. 'C'mon, Olly!' he called over
his shoulder. 'If we hurry now, we might just catch

the end of the Eel-Barrow Race at the village hall.'
He came to a halt and his shoulders slumped. 'You've
gone into the ship, haven't you, Olly?' he said. There
was no answer. Anton turned, and Olly was nowhere
to be seen.

'Anton!' he said aloud to himself. 'You are *not* going
into that ship! I strictly forbid it!' He stood stubbornly
by himself for a moment as a nervous fidget began in
his fingers. Then he suddenly broke into a sprint back
towards the ship. 'I'm coming!' he yelled. 'Wait for me!'

Olly had smelled some bad odours in his time. The
mess that the school guinea pig had made in their
headteacher's lap when he had that belly bug. The block
of cheese that Olly had hidden in the glovebox of his
parents' car and forgotten about. Worst of all, the stench
of the Brain-Drain concocted by Madame Strang at her
academy last summer. But the *Captain's Revenge* stank. It
stunk. It stinked. It stonk.

As Olly's eyes slowly but surely adjusted to the
darkness, he carefully picked his way along a narrow
passage, following the sound of Riz's footsteps ahead of
him. He could hardly stand up straight in the cramped
space, and he promptly banged his head on a metal pipe

in front of him. The pipe shivered, sending metallic cackles rippling into the gloom of the corridor ahead.

'Riz!' he called into the dark. 'Riz! Drew! Wait for me!'

Enormous curtains of seaweed hung from the wooden boards above his head, dripping ice-cold droplets of slime onto his face and down the back of his neck. A thick aroma of rotting fish hit him as a gust of wind rattled through the ship. Olly pressed his hand over his mouth and felt his stomach turn.

'Riz?' he called again. 'Do you see anything?'

A hand suddenly clamped down on his shoulder, and he yelped in fright.

'It's me!' whispered Riz.

'You scared the life out of me!' Olly hissed, poking into the darkness where he assumed her ribs would be.

'Ouch! That was my knee!' Riz replied angrily.

'Let me try again. I'll get your ribs this time!' Olly countered.

She shushed him and pointed down the passageway ahead of them. 'Drew's down here. Where's Anton?'

'He'll be here at any ... ARGH! MY BUM!'

'It's me!' came Anton's voice. 'Sorry, I meant to poke your shoulder.'

'Right, that's enough poking for the day,' Olly replied. 'Let's find Drew.'

Hurried footsteps sounded straight ahead of them.

'Drew!' called Riz. 'Drew, wait there. We're coming!'

The sound of a door slamming shut made them jump, but they were determined to keep going. They carefully continued down the passage and made their way deeper into the ship. The ceiling became lower and lower, and the stink of fish and rotting wood grew stronger as they picked their way over broken floorboards and slippery patches of seaweed.

Buuudumph.

The three children froze.

'What—' began Riz.

Buuudumph.

'What is that?' whispered Anton in a high squeak.

A slow and steady banging echoed its way down the ship towards them every few seconds, like a loud heartbeat.

Buuudumph.

'Do you think Drew is trying to break into something?' suggested Olly quietly.

Riz peered into the darkness ahead of them. 'I can't see anything,' she whispered back.

'Would you like a torch?' said Olly suddenly.

Riz looked at him in disbelief. 'You've had a torch this whole time?'

'Erm, maybe,' he said guiltily and rummaged through his rucksack. 'The batteries are low, though,' he told her as he passed her the torch and she flicked it on.

The beam danced over the ceiling above them, which was covered in an endless array of shells suckered to the wood. Riz shone the torch down the passageway.

'Dreeeew!' she called. But her voice bounced back as if it were mocking her. Drew didn't answer.

Buuudumph.

'It's coming from this way!' she told Olly and Anton.

They marched on towards the sound, Anton trailing nervously behind and peeking anxiously over his shoulder every few steps.

Finally, they arrived at the source of the sound – a heavy oak door, swinging in the wind and clattering off the wooden wall. A grimy padlock that had been keeping it shut now hung uselessly from the frame.

'Drew must have come in this way,' muttered Riz, shining the torch through the door. Another low-ceilinged passageway lay ahead, the floorboards shimmering with damp.

A sudden, sharp dog-whistle ripped down the corridor, beckoning them to hurry up.

'It's Drew!' said Olly with a relieved sigh. 'He's down there!'

Riz looked doubtfully at the padlock, then on down the passageway.

Anton elbowed his way past Riz and Olly and pulled the door fully open. 'Let's go!'

Riz hesitated for a moment. Something didn't feel quite right. There was an alarm bell ringing deep inside her. 'I don't know if this is a good idea,' she said suddenly. 'Something's not right.'

Another whistle shrieked down the hallway.

'Coming, Drew!' called Anton, happily trotting towards the sound.

'Where's he off to?' came a voice from behind Olly, who jumped and turned round.

'Oh, Drew. There you are,' he said, relieved.

Drew was standing beside him, a puzzled look on his face.

'Thank heavens you're here,' Olly told him. 'Anton's on his way to . . .' His voice trailed off and he stared at Drew in horror. 'Uh-oh,' he gasped.

'ANTON!' yelled Riz, throwing herself through the door and racing down the passageway towards the sound of Anton's footsteps. 'ANTON! COME BACK!' She hadn't got very far before she slipped on a wad of seaweed and crashed to the floor. 'It's not Drew!' she shouted, trying to haul herself upright. 'It's not DREW!'

An Anton-shaped blur was suddenly sprinting back down the corridor towards her, his eyes wide with terror. 'Run!' he yelled, pushing Riz to her feet and hurtling back to Drew and Olly. 'RUUUUN!'

No one asked questions. They galloped back down the passage as fast as the slick floor would allow. Riz's stomach swooped as she lost her balance again, landing on the floorboards with a hard thud. The air ballooned out of her lungs, and she struggled to catch her breath. Gasping for oxygen, she twisted round to look back down the hallway and couldn't believe her eyes.

A shape was dragging itself down the passage towards her – a bloated mess of scabby flesh and wriggling seaweed. It looked to have once been a man – a tall, long-haired sailor with broad shoulders and a limp. Now, its face was puffed up in a grotesque mass of leathery flesh, crawling with limpets and sea urchins. Its clothes, rotted and sopping wet, were draped with dirty seaweed, and a long-rusted sword swung at its side.

Where the creature's eyes

had once been, now there were only two black sockets, and its jaws yawned open, revealing two rows of jet-black teeth. A terrible screech burst from its mouth, a wail that ricocheted off the walls, and it made Riz feel like her eardrums were about to burst.

She lay frozen in terror on the floor, watching in disbelief as the creature hauled itself ever closer to her. She could smell it now too – a horrible stench of decay forcing its way inside her nostrils. The creature may not have had eyes, but it had certainly seen her, and it was coming for her, faster and faster with every crooked limp.

Suddenly, Riz was yanked backwards.

'C'mon, Riz!' It was Drew's voice. 'Run!'

She managed to tear her eyes away from the monster and dragged herself to her feet. Dancing around the globs of seaweed, Riz and Drew raced back down the passage towards the sound of Olly's and Anton's shouts. With every step she took, Riz expected an icy grip to clamp round her ankle and triumphantly drag her back into the darkness of the ship, but it never came.

They finally came to the hole they'd climbed through and burst out into the grey sunlight of Bony Beach. They dashed towards the dunes and their bikes, not waiting for the creature to emerge out of the hole. Pedalling hard away from the ship, they didn't stop for breath until they'd reached the outskirts of Snoops Bay and knew they were safe.

CHAPTER TEN

'What did you see in there?' Olly demanded as they slid from their saddles and collapsed onto a bench outside Burpy Gumby's Fancy Dress Shop, gasping for breath.

Riz and Drew struggled to find the words to explain what they'd seen. They sat in stupefied silence as the Festiv-Eel crowds bustled all around them.

'You saw him, didn't you?' said Olly suddenly, his voice beginning to wobble with panic.

Riz and Drew eventually nodded, still struggling to believe it themselves.

'We saw Captain Huxley,' Drew told his friends.

Anton's eyebrows shot up in disbelief.

Riz scowled at him. 'We know what we saw on that ship!'

'You saw what on the ship?' came a gravelly rasp.

The four children yelled in fright, twisting round to see Brandish squeezing himself onto the bench beside them.

He was cradling Kourtney's bowl and slipped it onto Anton's lap. 'Hold on to Kourtney for a minute, will you?' he said gruffly and dabbed at his brow with his grimy handkerchief. He looked damp, like he'd been fished out of a pond. 'I've just had to catch a lobster that made a break for freedom in the kiddies' swimming pool.'

Brandish took Kourtney's bowl back from Anton and handed him the stained hankie. Anton looked down at it in horror. 'So, you've been back out to the *Captain's Revenge*, have you?' Brandish growled, lowering his voice and casting a suspicious glance at the crowd flowing around them. 'Rumour has it she's the right way up again.'

'It wasn't us!' protested Riz. 'We went back to ...' She caught Drew's eye and fell silent.

'To what?' Brandish snarled, his eyes darting between Riz and Drew. 'To look for the treasure?'

'We didn't need to look,' Olly admitted over Riz's shoulder. 'We ... I ... accidentally took a golden coin when I collected some of the muck from around the ship. We think that's what caused the curse.'

'Please don't tell our parents!' pleaded Riz. 'We went back to the ship to return it as soon as we realized, and . . . well . . .' She fell silent and stared at her feet, her face growing red. She glanced up at Brandish again, expecting a thunderous expression, but instead his eyes were encouraging her to continue.

'I won't tell anyone,' he said quietly. 'You four have got the spirit of adventure in you. I have it myself – I'm a pirate, for Blackbeard's sake!' The friends sighed in relief. 'Tell me what happened,' he said gently.

So they told Brandish the whole story – how they'd returned to the ship, noticed track marks on the beach, heard weird noises inside the ship, and finally had a horrible encounter with a seaweed creature in the belly of the boat. He listened intently, absent-mindedly curling his hair round his finger as they spoke and giving the occasional casual nod to curious passers-by. When they'd finished and fallen into silence, Brandish plucked a tub of fish food from his coat and gently tapped a few crumbs into Kourtney's bowl. She ignored them.

'Well, youngsters,' rasped Brandish finally. 'You were lucky to escape with your lives and livers intact. The undead spirit that haunts that ship is as dangerous as any living pirate, and thirsty for revenge!'

'Revenge on who?' squeaked Olly.

Brandish shrugged. 'If anyone goes near that ship, they'll bring about the doom of Snoops Bay. Nobody's safe.' His eyes fell upon Mayor Turbot, who'd appeared in the throng of people, handing out cooked oysters and lemon wedges from an enormous tray. Tiara followed closely behind, snapping photographs and snapping at people to get out of her way.

'Press!' she declared loudly. 'Make way for *GossWorld*'s editor-in-chief!'

Olly rolled his eyes. 'There's the mayor!' He pointed. 'We need to talk to him and tell him what we saw!'

'He's a slippery fish, that one,' warned Brandish, giving the mayor a dark look. 'You be careful what you tell him. He'll find a way to make money out of it!'

Anton turned to Drew. 'I'm still waiting for an apology, by the way.'

'An apology for what?' his brother snapped back.

'Oh, let me think,' Anton replied sarcastically. 'For not believing that the *Captain's Revenge* curse is real. For dragging me back out to Bony Beach. For climbing inside that rotting old ship and putting us all in danger. For—'

'ALL RIGHT!' shouted Drew. 'I get the picture! Do you even think the mayor will believe us?'

'Well, we won't know if we don't tell him,' said Riz doubtfully.

'There you are, Brandish!' the mayor jumped in, coming to a sudden stop that made his wig wobble. 'I've been looking all over for you. My wife Frugal is planning to make her world-famous pickled trout pie for Keith and Judith's ceremony.'

'Sounds delicious,' muttered Riz to Drew, who smirked.

'It's world-famous,' Tiara told her coldly.

'It's in the *Guinness World Records*, as a matter of fact!' the mayor bragged.

'Yes, under the largest number of people to get food poisoning simultaneously,' snorted Brandish. 'Quite an explosive event last year, wasn't it, Mayor Turbot?'

The mayor blushed. 'Anyway,' he continued, 'I need fifty of your juiciest trout by tomorrow morning.'

'That's not going to be possible. So very sorry,' said Brandish, not looking the least bit sorry. He reached for the mayor's steaming tray of oysters and took a handful.

'No trout in stock – there's a shortage. But I won't bore you with the details.'

'No, please don't!' snapped the mayor, leaning in closer. Olly wrinkled his nose at the smell of his breath. 'You *will* deliver fifty trout to my wife's kitchen tonight. Got it, Brandish?' His eyes glared into Brandish's, daring him to say no.

The old sea captain stared back, snapping open his oyster shell with a *crack* and squeezing a few drops of lemon juice on top of it. 'Is there cod liver oil in your ears, mayor? We are out of *trout*.'

'We'll see about that!' hissed the mayor, before turning sharply on his heel and disappearing back into the crowd.

Brandish grimaced. 'A right rudder-faced rascal, that one! Truth be told, I have lots of trout.' He raised the oyster to his mouth and gulped it down in one go. 'Crack 'em open. It's a Festiv-Eel tradition,' commanded Brandish as he offered the remaining oysters to the children. 'One quick twist and straight down the gullet!'

Drew gave his oyster a hard twist. It snapped open, revealing gooey insides the colour of snot. 'I've lost my appetite.' He winced.

Brandish gave an ear-splitting guffaw. 'I promise

they're delicious!' He fixed Riz with a mischievous smirk. 'Go on. I dare you, missy!'

Riz had very few rules in life, but one of them was to never turn down a dare. She returned Brandish's steely gaze. 'Aye, aye, cap'n!' She cracked her oyster open, clamped her eyes tightly shut and raised it to her mouth.

'STOP!' Olly suddenly grabbed Riz's wrist, staring in disbelief at the oyster she'd been about to swallow. He snatched it from her and emptied it into his palm.

'Ew, Olly!' Riz shouted. 'What are you playing at?'

Olly carefully plucked something from the oyster and gave it a shake, sending droplets of slime everywhere.

Brandish's eyes widened in amazement. 'What in the name of Poseidon's pitchfork is that?'

'It's a note,' gasped Olly, looking at Riz.

'Another one?' squeaked Anton, leaping from the bench in fright. 'Is it from Huxley?'

Olly held the tightly rolled scrap of paper as if it was about to bite him. 'Maybe it would be better to ignore it . . .'

'Don't be silly,' said Drew impatiently, taking the note from his pal and unravelling it.

The four friends and Brandish craned over Drew's

shoulder to read what was written on the paper. Scribbled in huge green letters were the words: IF YOU COME WITHIN 100 METRES OF MY SHIP, YOU WILL BE DOOMED.

'WE'RE DOOMED!' Anton shrieked, falling to his knees.

'Quieten down,' shushed Brandish. 'Someone might hear you!'

Riz, Olly and Drew looked at each other in stunned silence, their mouths flapping open and shut like fish.

'Do you believe in the curse now, Drew?' cried Anton.

Olly, who had managed to compose himself, took the note from Drew's hands and studied it. He held it up to the fading sunlight and frowned.

'Olly?' asked Drew. 'What are you thinking?'

Olly had stuck his tongue out of the side of his mouth, as he often did when he was concentrating. 'I'm thinking,' he muttered, almost to himself, 'about how strange it is that a three-hundred-year-old pirate would use metres . . .'

'What are you talking about?' Anton paused his hysterics.

A faint smile spread across Olly's face and he turned to the fishmonger. 'Captain Brandish, would you hand me that slice of lemon, please?'

Brandish looked at him quizzically but handed the lemon wedge over. Olly began to delicately squeeze the juice onto the note, allowing it to stain the paper.

'Pirates in 1723 didn't use metres,' he continued, his voice growing louder and more confident. 'They used miles – nautical miles, to be precise.'

'So . . .' Riz stared at the lemon juice, utterly confused. 'You don't think Huxley wrote this note?'

'Metres weren't introduced until seventy years after Huxley's death,' Olly told her, keeping his eyes firmly fixed on the paper. 'So he wouldn't have known what they were. Someone else wrote this note to scare us, which means they probably wrote the note we found at the ship too.'

'But what's with the lemon juice?' Drew asked, wondering if Olly had lost his mind. 'You're not going to eat the paper, are you?'

'Lemon juice reveals secrets,' Olly told him, flapping the paper in the sunshine to dry it off. 'It's been used for hundreds of years as invisible ink.' He spread the note flat across his palm. The group leant in close. They could now make out some other marks on the paper – faint scrawls that were becoming more visible as the lemon juice dried.

'But it can do more than that,' Olly continued, narrowing his eyes. 'If this note was written in a notepad and the page was torn out, the lemon juice might be able to show us what else was written on previous pages, especially if the writer was leaning down hard on the pen.'

'Oh, my giddy guppy!' Brandish was staring in amazement at the paper as the scrawls became more and more apparent by the second. 'What does it say?'

Olly held the paper up to the sunlight again, a broad grin spreading across his face. 'Well, I think we can safely say Huxley didn't write this note,' he said finally. 'And I've got a pretty good idea who did.'

CHAPTER ELEVEN

'Did anyone else have nightmares last night?' whispered Anton.

'Yeah, I dreamt you were farting in your sleep,' Drew told him. 'Oh, wait, that wasn't a dream!'

'Keep quiet back there!' barked the voice of Squid O'Malley. The four friends jumped in fright and quit talking.

It was the next morning: the day of the Snoops Bay aquarium all-access tour. The four children had crammed themselves into a coughing old bus, packed in like sardines with dozens of eager locals and tourists who had nothing better to do, and they were now on their way to the second event of the Festiv-Eel.

The town was heaving with people, the pavements already packed, and a band had struck up in the square, merrily tooting out sea shanties to an eager crowd of onlookers. On either side of the main street, buildings seemed to sag under the weight of streamers, bunting, balloons and homemade signs flapping in the sea breeze.

'Operation Crown Jewels is a GO!' hissed Olly to Riz as the bus wheezed to a stop.

'Roger that,' Riz muttered, giving Drew and Anton a nod as they stepped off the bus. They in turn gave two quick salutes.

No sooner had they landed on the pavement than a familiar voice sounded behind them. 'VIP coming through! Out of the way!' Tiara barked. '*GossWorld* is getting an exclusive with Squid O'Malley about her latest sea creature.' She stuck her tongue out at Olly.

'Is that so?' came another voice, this time making them all jump. Brandish was limping towards them. 'You weren't very nice about me in this morning's *GossWorld*!'

Tiara smirked and yanked a pristine copy of the magazine out of her bag. 'Hold this!' she ordered Brandish rudely, shoving her bag into his chest and nearly knocking him sideways.

Tiara opened the magazine and unfolded an enormous three-page spread. Over an unflattering photograph of Brandish and Kourtney the blobfish was a headline in giant letters: **EXCLUSIVE! BARMY BRANDISH'S PLOT TO RUIN FESTIV-EEL!** A smaller photo of Riz, Olly, Drew and Anton was stuck in the corner over the caption: *Brandish's make-believe fairy tales fooled these notorious losers!*

'Fancy a copy, Riz?' Tiara grinned. Riz took a threatening step towards her, but Brandish pulled her back and threw Tiara's bag at her feet.

'On your way, girl,' he growled.

Tiara tittered and marched away, elbowing herself to the front of the queue outside the aquarium.

The four friends, along with Brandish, made their way into the building and were soon stood with a crowd of people in front of an enormous tank covered by a huge tarpaulin. Squid O'Malley appeared, to rapturous applause, before clearing her throat for attention.

'I bet you're all wondering what's behind this sheet,' Squid told the onlookers airily. 'Well, in a matter of seconds, you'll have the pleasure of seeing an incredible specimen that's come straight off the plane from Mozambique. Count yourselves very lucky – not many people in the world have witnessed what you're about to.'

There was complete silence as Squid reached up to the tarpaulin and grabbed hold of the corner. She yanked it hard, and the audience gasped. Countless pairs of perfectly round eyeballs were staring out from the tank. They bulged like white-hot boils, ready to burst atop dozens of huge bulbous red heads that pulsed with the motion of the water. The tank was swimming with octopuses – a vast forest of twisting tentacles, bristling with suckers, that clung to the glass. Their eyes fixed the crowd with cruel stares.

'Behold!' crowed Squid, gazing up in admiration at the tank. 'One of the rarest sea creatures in existence, right in front of your very eyes!'

'What are they?' cooed Tiara, pressing her face flat against the glass. Squid shooed her backwards with a swing of her whip.

'Don't touch the glass!' she snapped. 'You *don't* want to anger them.' A collective gulp rippled through the crowd.

'They don't look very happy to be in that tank,' Olly said to Riz.

Squid continued with her spiel. 'These creatures are known as the *kraken abominus*, or in English, the abominable octopus! Each one is the size of a large dog and possesses the suction power of eight hundred vacuum cleaners. This is the only species of octopus on the entire planet known to attack and devour –' she paused for dramatic effect – 'humans!' Horrified chatter filled the air. 'This mollusc is the first of the many monstrous sea creatures that will soon be housed in Snoops Bay aquarium.' With a flourish, Squid pulled a handful of limp fish from her coat pocket and tossed them up onto the grille of the tank. 'This is their favourite dinner,' she told the crowd. 'Lightly salted Albanian sea bass, rubbed in garlic butter.'

The sea bass lay there, their glassy eyes frozen open in shock. 'Observe as they feed!' she bellowed.

The room fell deathly silent. The octopuses had noticed the fish above their heads, and for a few moments they stayed completely still, their enormous eyes watching for any hint of movement. Then, without warning, they struck. Hundreds of tentacles, like terrible bolts of lightning, flashed through the water and erupted through the bars of the grille. The fish disappeared in a slithering mountain of flesh, before the tentacles plunged back into the water. The tank was suddenly one huge, bubbling feeding frenzy as the octopuses feasted on their breakfast.

Minutes later, the fish skeletons, picked entirely clean of flesh, sank down to the bottom of the tank.

The crowd burst into deafening applause, and Squid took a bow.

'Make it do something else!' Tiara shouted.

'Yeah!' commanded a red-haired boy in the front row. 'Do they do tricks?'

Shouts of agreement broke out, until the crowd began to chant and clap in unison. 'DO A TRICK! DO A TRICK! DO A TRICK!'

Squid silenced the audience with a snap of her whip and glared at them menacingly. 'These are wild animals,' she hissed. 'Their fangs could purée a whole cow in thirty seconds flat! Their suckers could lift a car! They don't do *tricks*!'

Olly turned to look at his three friends. 'Let's put Operation Crown Jewels into action now, while everyone's distracted!' he whispered.

Riz threw a quick glance at the crowd and nodded. 'Roger that.'

Elbowing his way to the front, Anton positioned himself next to Tiara, who was busy snapping pictures of the twisting vortex of octopuses.

'Out of the shot, you drip!' she snapped at him. 'This is going to be the front page of *GossWorld*!'

'My sincere apologies, Tiara.' Anton folded himself into an almost-curtsey, a sickly-sweet smile painted across his face. 'Wouldn't you like to be in the picture too? I can take a photo of you and the krakens, if you like?'

'Good idea.' Tiara shoved her camera into Anton's hands and strode over to the tank. But as she spun round, ready to strike a pose, she stopped dead. Anton was scuttling down a long glass corridor towards the aquarium's atrium.

'OI!' yelled Tiara, flinging herself after him. 'Get back here with my camera, you thief!'

Anton disappeared to the left, through a thick metal door marked: FISH FOOD. He slammed it tightly shut behind him, but with a furious snarl, Tiara wrenched it open again. The room was pitch black, and a sour, musty smell filled the air.

'Where on earth . . . ?' Tiara spluttered, before two sets of hands grabbed hold of her. She squealed in fright as the lights flicked on.

'Keep quiet!' hissed Riz. 'Or you'll be sleeping with the fishes!'

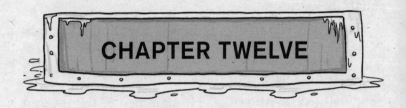

CHAPTER TWELVE

'What are you doing?' Tiara wriggled to try to free herself from Drew's and Anton's grasp.

The five children were standing in the centre of a vast chamber. Great swathes of freezing fog prowled along the stone floor, nipping at their ankles. The chamber was, in fact, more like a dungeon – a deep room that stretched out in all directions under a dripping rock ceiling. Ice shimmered with an eerie blue glow across every surface, and the walls bristled with icicles. A heavy brass lamp, flickering and shivering in the cold, was set into the ceiling. It cast long shadows yawning into the darkness, curling and distorting in the mist that carpeted the floor. In the very centre of the room stood a set of enormous freezers, humming quietly and packed with what looked like ready meals, waiting to be unwrapped and fed to the

aquarium's sea life. 'Reef Stroganoff,' read one. 'Mac & Seas,' said another.

'What's going on here?' Tiara backed into a corner, away from their accusing glares.

'We'll ask the questions, Tiara!' Olly brandished a scrap of paper accusingly at her. 'Recognize this?' he demanded.

Tiara glanced guiltily at the note, then looked back to Olly. 'I've never seen it before in my life!'

'Listen, Tiara,' Anton said menacingly. 'We can do this the easy way, or the hard way. Either you confess of your own free will, or else . . .' A long pause followed.

Tiara twisted round to look at him, her eyes wide with fear. 'Or else what?' she stammered.

Anton gave a sheepish shrug. 'Actually, we haven't thought that far.'

'We know this is yours!' Olly interrupted, sticking the paper in front of Tiara's face. 'Whoever wrote it also had a shopping list for Burpy Gumby's Fancy Dress Shop in the same notebook, and you're his best customer. You've been trying to scare us to keep the story of the *Captain's Revenge* all for yourself!'

'And you were the one in charge of the iced-tea stand

at the pool yesterday,' added Drew. 'You had the perfect opportunity to pour seawater into those cups.'

'Rubbish,' Tiara declared. 'You can't prove that! Anyone could have written a shopping list for Burpy Gumby's.'

'*You* wrote it.' Olly's eyes narrowed. 'And you misspelled "DOOM", too.'

'No, I didn't!' snapped Tiara, stiffening with indignation. Realizing her blunder, she gasped.

'No, you didn't!' crowed Anton. 'We got you to confess though!'

'What I meant to say was, if I had written the note, I wouldn't have misspelled anything,' Tiara said quickly, reddening under the group's gleeful gazes. Finally, she slumped in defeat. 'Okay, fine!' she snapped. 'I put that note in the oyster. I was just trying to keep my exclusive story from you amateurs!'

'It's not *your* exclusive!' Olly told her. 'It's *our* exclusive!'

'That's beside the point. Drew. Anton. Let her go,' Riz sighed, and the brothers reluctantly relaxed their grip.

Tiara pulled away from them haughtily. 'If I have permanent arm damage, my daddy will sue your daddy!' She sniffed.

'Listen, Tiara.' Riz took a deep breath. 'Something strange has been happening in Snoops Bay since the *Captain's Revenge* was discovered. And if we want to figure it out, then we have to work together!'

'What are you talking about?' snapped Tiara, still massaging her arms.

'We saw ...' Olly began, then caught himself. 'Riz and Drew *say* they saw a zombie down at the *Captain's Revenge*. The zombie of Captain Horatio Huxley.'

Tiara let out a sudden guffaw. 'A *what*?'

'We *did* see it!' Drew said firmly. 'We saw a zombie pirate, or something that looked a lot like it!'

'Did you see anything when you were at the ship?' Olly asked Tiara. 'Anyone hanging around, or anything that looked suspicious?'

'Unlike you, I haven't been anywhere near that ship,' Tiara said, her voice rising. 'My daddy said it was off limits, remember?'

Olly frowned. 'Yes, you have! You obviously left the first note as well. The one that told us to bury the ship.'

Tiara shook her head. 'I *told* you, it's off limits!'

'No, that can't be,' muttered Olly, rooting in his pockets and plucking out the note from the ship. 'You must have written this note too – look.' He stuffed the note into her hand.

Tiara looked down at the scrap of paper. 'Oh ...' she murmured, almost to herself. 'Oh, wow.'

'What?' Riz demanded. 'So you've seen it before?'

'Yes, but not because I left it by the ship.' Tiara looked up, a nervous smile appearing on her face. 'In fact, I've seen lots of these before.' She cast her eyes round the group. 'This isn't a note, it's a receipt. I've got loads just like it.' She suddenly started to rummage in her pocket.

Riz exchanged an uncertain glance with Olly. 'A receipt for what?'

'For this!' Tiara had plucked a crumpled receipt from her pocket and was now uncurling it. She held it up beside the note from the ship. 'The water has washed away most of the writing,' she said. 'But it's identical.'

'Oops,' whispered Anton quietly. 'We may have jumped to conclusions.'

'No.' Riz whipped round to him. 'Drew and I saw a zombie!'

'You saw what *looked* like a zombie!' Olly interrupted hotly. 'Someone must have paid a visit to Burpy's dressed up like a zombie and left the receipt at the ship! They've been pulling our legs to keep us away from the *Captain's Revenge* and the treasure.'

'More than one person!' Anton reminded him. 'There was one set of footprints and two bike tracks at the ship, remember?'

'And I bet the same person laced the iced tea with seawater.' Olly furrowed his brow.

'My tea!' Tiara suddenly scowled, and her hands flew to her hips. 'That's a step too far,' she growled. 'Terrorize a community, send children threatening notes – fine. But when you sabotage an iced beverage – ' her eyes narrowed to slits – 'that means war!'

'But who could it be?' Riz was utterly exasperated. Every answer they found posed more questions.

Tiara stuffed the receipt back into her pocket. 'We need to go to Burpy's,' she said finally, her face brightening.

'He'll have a record of all the costumes his customers have bought. If we can look at those, we'll know who's been running around dressed as a pirate zombie!'

'These people must really want the town to steer clear of the *Captain's Revenge*,' Olly insisted. 'That way they'll have time to find the treasure and take it for themselves. But if Tiara hasn't been near the ship like we thought she had, who else could it be?'

'No one else has been there,' said Anton glumly. 'Except for Squid O'Malley.'

'Squid!' Olly's mouth dropped open. 'Of course!'

'Squid?' Drew was staring at him in confusion. 'What's she got to do with this?'

Olly was suddenly pacing – something he often did when his brain was popping into gear. 'We know Squid's been to the ship because she was the one who told the town about it.'

'So?' scoffed Drew. 'What about the seawater in the tea? Squid wasn't anywhere near the drinks stand!'

'Yes, she was!' The words burst from Riz's mouth. 'She went over to the table for an iced tea as soon as she arrived.' She opened her eyes wide, staring around at her friends. 'She could have poured seawater into the jug. And don't you remember she crushed her cup before she'd even taken a sip of the drink?'

'That still doesn't explain the zombie we saw.' Drew shivered. 'Do you really think Squid dressed up as Huxley to scare people away from the treasure?'

'Wait a minute!' Tiara pulled her satchel from her back and started scrabbling through it. 'I was taking photographs at the opening and I got them printed out for *GossWorld*!'

'And?' said Olly, rolling his eyes. 'We don't have time for a sneak preview, Tiara.'

Tiara ignored him and upended her satchel, scattering its contents onto the damp floor. 'What if I accidentally caught the culprit in the act?'

Drew considered this, then shrugged at Olly. 'She may have a point!'

'Where ... is it ... ?' Tiara fell to her knees, searching desperately for something. 'My *GossWorld* dossier!' She looked up at the group in horror. 'It's gone!'

'What's a dossier?' Anton frowned at her.

'It's a fancy word for folder,' Olly told him. 'But what do you mean, Tiara?' he demanded.

'It's not here!' she shrilled, her voice quivering in panic. 'Someone's taken it!'

CHAPTER THIRTEEN

The door behind them was suddenly thrown open and the five children squeaked in fright.

'What is going on here?' Squid O'Malley was standing in the doorway, a furious look on her face. 'This section of the aquarium is *strictly* off limits!' She marched over to Tiara's satchel and began to stuff the girl's belongings back into it. 'Take this and clear off!' she ordered them, tossing the bag to Tiara with a growl.

The five of them gabbled apologies and filed out past Squid, trying to avoid her thunderous glare. They scurried back to the crowd, who were still gathered round the enormous octopus tank where the krakens were glowering through the glass.

Suddenly, Olly wrinkled his nose in disgust. 'Do you

smell garlic?' He turned to Riz. 'Someone didn't brush their teeth this morning ...'

Riz scowled at him, but her face quickly dropped when a sudden *bang* boomed around the aquarium like a clap of thunder. The sound had come from the tank – one of the krakens had collided with the wall. Where the glass was once smooth, a thin crack had appeared and a tiny stream of water was now leaking out and pitter-pattering onto the tiles.

As the crowd watched in horror, a second spidery crack spread from the first, and then a third. The drip became a dribble, then a flow, then a gush, and soon water was lapping hungrily at the feet of the people gathered around the tank.

In the deathly silence, Squid took a single step forward, her eyes never leaving the leak. Her hand slowly snaked down and gripped one of several whips hanging from her belt. 'Nobody ... move ...' she breathed, her face now deathly white.

The cloud of creatures inside the tank had started to swarm together, drifting down eagerly towards the crack. A curious sucker darted out to investigate the cobweb of splinters and gently pressed against the glass. Then another tentacle shot out. And another.

They're testing it, Riz thought, a wave of terror washing through her body like icy seawater. She tried to take a step away from the tank, but it felt like her legs were set in concrete. She couldn't move.

Squid, on the other hand, was inching towards the tank, her hand on her whip. 'They want to feed again,' she said in a low, warning voice. 'They've caught a scent.'

Next to Riz, Olly scrunched up his nose again as another whiffy wave of garlic hit him. This time, Riz could smell it, and an awful realization suddenly hit her. 'The garlic sea bass!' she breathed. She whirled around to face the rest of the onlookers. 'Everyone, check your pockets and bags! Someone here is a walking piece of kraken bait!'

Tiara looked puzzled. 'Check them for what?'

'Check them now!' Riz yelled. 'Before the krakens come for you!'

Tiara frowned but copied the rest of the crowd. Suddenly, her look of confusion twisted into panic as she dug deep into her bag, her fingers closing round something wet and slippery. 'Uh-oh,' she whispered, pulling out the limp shape of a sea bass, smeared in garlic butter. 'I think they might be after this?'

'GET RID OF THAT!' roared Riz, dashing towards Tiara and swiping it out of her hand. The fish arced up in the air and they watched in horror as it landed with a greasy *thwack* in front of the tank.

'Don't,' whispered Squid, 'you dare . . .'

But it was too late. The swarm of krakens began to ram themselves against the side of the tank, and dozens more cracks bloomed across the glass. The crowd gasped in fright and started to squirm.

Squid threw an arm back towards them. 'No one move!' she hissed, now rooted to the spot herself. 'Don't move a muscle!'

BOOM. The krakens attacked the glass again, and the tank moaned in protest. *BOOM. BOOM. BOOM.*

'EVERYONE!' yelled Squid, whirling round to face the crowd. 'RUN!'

The onlookers immediately began to flee, but at the sound of Squid's words, it was as if a hundred cannons had fired all at once. Every tentacle rammed into the glass, and the screws and rivets that had been holding the tank together gave way. The front panel was blown outwards, and a huge wave crashed towards Tiara, who was still near the tank. She fell to the floor with a petrified scream.

Squid's hand shot out like a bullet, and her whip sliced through the air. The end latched itself round Tiara's ankle and tugged her backwards, yanking her away from the tsunami that was about to consume her. But as the water poured out, so too did the krakens . . .

CHAPTER FOURTEEN

The octopuses suckered themselves onto the tiles of the aquarium, huffing great sprays of saltwater into the air and flapping their mouths wide open. Pandemonium descended as the locals and tourists of Snoops Bay stumbled and tripped over each other to get away from the tide of water and flailing tentacles spreading across the floor.

Riz was swept up in the surge of people running for the exit. She almost lost her balance and fought to stay upright. Drew yelled her name from somewhere in the crowd, and she twisted round to try to find his face but couldn't spot him or Anton through the masses. Brandish was trying to shove his way through the stampede towards the tank, bellowing at the top of his voice to be let through. Olly suddenly appeared beside her, his clothes wringing wet and clinging to his body.

'I got sprayed!' he spluttered into her ear. 'Let's get out of here!'

'Great idea, Olly,' she shouted back sarcastically. 'I would never have thought of that!'

The crack of Squid's whip resounded around the aquarium. She was rooted to the spot, encircled by the seething sea of krakens, which seemed to be crowding around her, surrounding her from every angle. The large black octopus who seemed to be leading the charge slithered suddenly in front of her. Its head jabbed forward like lightning, and its jaws snapped inches away from Squid's ankles. She twisted out of the way with a split second to spare, and threw her arms out wide, making herself look as big as possible in the face of the creatures.

'Back!' she commanded, snapping her whip down hard on the tiles, cracking the porcelain with a sound like a gunshot. 'BACK, ALL OF YOU!'

The black kraken reared its head and jets of steaming water gushed like fountains from its ear holes. It roared, a bawling sound that made the windows of the aquarium rattle, and more screams erupted from the crowd.

Meanwhile, people continued to dash through the emergency fire doors at the far end of the aquarium, bursting out into the sunlight and sprinting for safety. Riz spotted a boy climbing to his feet from the floor, a mop of red sodden hair smeared across his scalp. He was hanging on desperately to the T-shirt of a taller boy with dark hair.

'Anton! Drew!' shouted Riz, gasping in relief.

Drew turned at the sound of his name, looking just as relieved to see her. 'Riz! Let's get out of here!'

'That's what I said!' yelled Olly over Riz's shoulder.

'Help!' came a sudden cry.

In Squid's haste to control the krakens, she'd completely forgotten to help Tiara to her feet. The four friends turned and noticed her still on the floor, frozen in panic. But this time the tentacles of a kraken had slithered round her ankle, and they were squeezing tighter and tighter as she tried to kick herself free.

'Drop her!' commanded Squid. The kraken just roared and moved closer to Tiara.

'HELP!' she shouted, hammering hard on the slimy suckers with her bare hands. 'Someone, help me!'

Without thinking, Riz began to sprint back towards Tiara.

'Riz, come back!' Olly called to her.

The world suddenly jumped into fast forward, and Riz found herself sprinting towards the wriggling girl on the tiles. She leapt past Squid and dived headfirst towards Tiara. A deafening *whoosh* sounded as a tentacle whizzed over Riz's head, close enough for her to feel a few salty droplets splat onto her face. The kraken had missed her by mere centimetres. She ducked down low and grabbed one of Tiara's arms.

'Kick as hard as you can!' she yelled.

'GET AWAY!' Squid barked, cracking her whips at the beastly creature.

Tiara yanked her left foot with a yell, and for a moment the octopus lost its grip. It roared in anger and sent more tentacles flying at them. One of them, icy cold, grabbed Riz round the waist. The words of Huxley's poem shot through her mind like a thunderbolt: 'The first day brings a salty sea, the next a terrible grip.'

She gasped and lost her balance as the freezing-cold suckers clung to her body, landing with a hard thump on the tiles. She was fish food.

'AWAY! AWAY, YE BRUTE!' Brandish was suddenly standing over Riz, swinging a swordfish at the kraken's bulbous head. The swordfish cut through the air and landed squarely between the creature's eyes, dazing it for a moment. It gave a squawk of surprise and furiously lunged for Brandish. He danced out of its way and swung down hard again, dealing it another thump.

'Get out of the way!' he bellowed to Riz as the octopus released her from its grip and focused its attention on Brandish.

'Captain Brandish!' shouted Squid. 'Watch your back!'

Brandish whipped round, grunting in surprise at the sight of another kraken wriggling its way towards him, fangs bared. 'No, you don't!' he yelled with a swipe of his swordfish, bonking the advancing octopus on the noggin and dodging out of the way. It squealed and recoiled, scurrying away with its legs between its legs.

The horde of sea creatures was finally retreating, driven backwards by Brandish with his swordfish and Squid with her whip. Riz and Tiara watched in astonishment as the octopuses began to skitter towards the ruins of their tank in a desperate attempt to escape the weapons.

'Someone call the mayor!' shouted Squid over her shoulder. 'And you five kids –' she stabbed an accusing finger straight at the group – 'stay right where you are!'

Riz, Olly, Drew, Anton and Tiara gulped.

CHAPTER FIFTEEN

The four friends stood in front of Mayor Turbot's enormous desk, staring intently at their shoes. Brandish was standing grimly by the door. Tiara was wrapped tightly in Brandish's leather trench coat, which was three times too big for her, staring straight ahead with a frazzled expression on her face. She'd only spoken one word since her close call with the octopus: 'sea bass'.

Tiara's dad had his head in his hands. He'd abandoned his wig and his bald patch was shiny with sweat that glinted in the light of his desk lamp. He finally raised his head and planted his palms on his desk, leaving a smear of perspiration across the leather surface. 'That's quite the tale,' he muttered before locking eyes with each member of the group in turn. 'Do you think it's funny to waste my time with cock-and-bull stories about pirate ships, mutant captains coming back from the dead for revenge and age-old curses?'

Brandish opened his mouth to interrupt.

'Quiet, captain!' snapped the mayor.

'Sea bass,' said Tiara quietly to herself.

'In fairness, Mayor Turbot,' Drew said meekly, 'Captain Huxley appeared more as a zombie than a mutant.'

'It doesn't matter what he appeared as,' Riz reminded them. 'Because either way someone has been trying to convince the town that the curse is real in order to scare everyone away from the ship. They want Huxley's treasure – whatever it is – all for themselves!'

'Who's this mysterious someone?' snapped the mayor. 'One minute you're convinced the curse is real, now you think it's a load of old tosh. If I didn't know better, I'd say you're trying to sabotage the Festiv-Eel!'

'We're telling the truth!' protested Riz, feeling her face turn red. 'You tasted the seawater in the iced tea yourself. Then bait turned up in Tiara's pocket so the krakens would attack. And we know at least three people have been to the *Captain's Revenge* searching for the treasure!'

Mayor Turbot looked uncertain for a moment. He shot a quick glance at his daughter, who was sitting unblinking in the corner, and then gathered himself. 'As far as I'm concerned, this is all your doing. The four of you are *banned* from attending the final Festiv-Eel event tomorrow. If I catch so much as a sniff of you near the harbour, you'll be sent to the police station quicker than you can say "clam chowder"! Do you understand?'

'Please, Mayor Turbot. Go down to the ship on Bony Beach and see for yourself!' urged Olly.

'No one goes near that ship!' he spat, placing his hands behind his back like a ship's captain patrolling the deck. 'By order of the mayor, Bony Beach is off limits! We'll see Keith and Judith off tomorrow afternoon, and then we'll deal with that ship. Until then, I want every police officer in Snoops Bay guarding the beach. No one goes in or out!'

The children's mouths clamped shut.

'Sea bass,' said Tiara, breaking the silence.

Mayor Turbot pinched the bridge of his nose. 'Captain Brandish will escort you home. Out!'

'Can I leave you a copy of *Unearthed*?' Olly asked suddenly, pulling a battered newspaper from his bag and laying it on the mayor's desk.

With a gargled roar, Mayor Turbot swiped his hand

across the desk, sending a fountain of paperwork flying across the room. 'OUT!' he bellowed, as Olly dived to retrieve his newspaper. 'And take your mucky paper with you!'

Brandish's fishmonger van was not roomy, and it took quite a lot of pushing, pulling and squashing for all four children to fit inside. The van had been sprayed with ugly blotches of blue, green and white – an illustration of sea life crudely painted on each side. Out of the mouth of a jolly-looking whale bloomed a huge speech bubble that said: *THE RED HERRING FISH EMPORIUM – O-FISH-ALLY THE BEST FISH IN SNOOPS BAY!'* And attached to the roof of the van was a colossal plastic swordfish, which had seen better days. Its white and navy paint was peeling, rust was beginning to gather on its belly and its long, spiked nose was badly bent out of shape.

Unsurprisingly, the inside stank of fish. Riz sat in the passenger seat and once she was strapped in, Brandish handed her Kourtney's fishbowl before twisting the ignition key. The van spluttered and coughed into life, sending clouds of fish-laced petrol into the air. Olly, Drew and Anton were perched on the back seats, all three of them gazing forlornly out of the window.

'It's so unfair,' muttered Olly, almost under his breath. 'No one believes us. We didn't even ask for any of this!'

'Captain Brandish believes us,' Riz told him in a cheery but unconvincing tone. 'Don't you, Captain Brandish?'

'The mayor is an idiot,' Brandish replied gruffly, flicking a switch under his steering wheel. A blast of static sounded from a speaker nailed to the roof of the van, and then it began to blare a scratchy recording of a jaunty sea shanty.

'Thou shalt have a fishy, on a little dishy, thou shalt have a fishy when the boat comes in!' warbled a voice in a high falsetto, sounding suspiciously like Brandish himself.

'Cheer up, shipmates!' he called back to his passengers, stamping on the accelerator.

The van jumped forward, and Riz barely managed to keep Kourtney's bowl from spilling over. The blobfish sat sadly inside, unperturbed by the sudden sloshing and jostling of her home.

Brandish sang along merrily with the music blasting from the speaker, swerving wildly all over the road and shouting nasty names at motorists honking their horns at him. Riz gripped onto Kourtney's bowl for dear life.

'Driving a van is a lot harder than a ship!' he yelled at the children over the music. 'There aren't as many pedestrians in the ocean!' He swerved to avoid a lollipop man and narrowly missed slamming into a traffic light. A green-faced Anton moaned in the back seat.

'You just went through a red light!' called Drew. 'And we told you Riz's house is the other way!'

'I get confused with directions that aren't port and starboard,' Brandish told him. 'Listen, kids.' His expression turned thoughtful. 'For all you know, Mayor Turbot could be the one behind this! Maybe he wants to get his grimy paws on the *Captain's Revenge*!'

'Mayor Turbot?' Olly frowned.

'I mean, it's not out of the question . . .' Drew replied. 'He might have even brought Tiara in on it too!'

'The girl who, at this very moment, can only say the word "sea bass"?' scoffed Riz. 'I hardly think she's a criminal mastermind, Drew.'

'Think about it!' Drew told the group, starting to gabble. 'Tiara could have poured seawater into her own iced tea on the first day of this so-called curse. She was the one who had fish in her pocket so that the krakens attacked on the second day. Who knows what she's got up her sleeve for the third day? And we don't know for certain that she *hasn't* been down to the ship.'

'But why would the mayor be behind it?' Riz asked Brandish. 'Why would he want people to think that Captain Horatio Huxley is back from the dead?'

Olly cleared his throat. 'I might have the answer to that.' He pulled a wad of paper from his pocket. 'I picked this up from the mayor's floor when I rescued my copy of *Unearthed*,' he told them, with more than a hint of smugness.

Gazing down at the paper, the children could see a blueprint design of a ship-shaped building, with measurements and arrows scrawled all over it.

'TOP SECRET!' Drew read aloud. 'First draft design of Full Scream Ahead, the world's first haunted shipping centre.'

'Shipping centre?' Anton frowned. 'Like a shopping centre?'

Drew continued. 'Captain Horatio Huxley and his crew of ghouls look forward to welcoming you to their salty lair.' Drew's eyebrows shot up. 'Walk the plank, then shop till you drop in our shipping centre, complete with restaurants, bars, cinema, bowling alley and ...' His eyebrows rose even higher. 'A car showroom.'

'He wants to turn the *Captain's Revenge* into a tourist

attraction!' spat Brandish, angrily honking his horn at nothing in particular. 'That land-lubbing, scally-wagging picaroon! That's why he wants the town to stay away from the ship!'

'What about Squid? She was the one who caught us in the aquarium's freezer room.' Anton shook his brother's shoulder hard. 'She picked up Tiara's things from the floor and put them in her bag. How do we know she didn't take that moment to plant the sea bass and send the krakens crazy?'

'We don't know.' Drew slumped in his seat.

'Don't forget about me, shipmates!' Brandish wagged a warning finger. Riz wished he'd keep his hands on the steering wheel.

'I'm a suspect too!' the old captain told them. 'In fact, everyone is a suspect!'

Riz frowned. 'You might be the only person who believes us, Captain Brandish!'

'If we can't trust you, who can we trust?' Olly looked worried.

'If a pirate's life has taught me anything,' Brandish said, 'it's that you can't trust anybody, especially a salt-soaked old scallywag like me. Don't forget that, and don't rule anybody out as a suspect, unless you're absolutely sure.'

A long silence followed, broken only by the caterwauling sea shanties on Brandish's radio.

'So what do we do now?' Anton was gazing glumly out of the window. 'I'd already chosen my outfit to wave off Keith and Judith tomorrow . . .'

'Don't worry,' Drew told his brother, giving him a reassuring pat on the knee, 'I'm sure there are lots of other events you can go to dressed as a karate-chopping prawn.'

'I spent three months' worth of pocket money in Burpy's!' Anton huffed dejectedly.

Riz's palm flew to her forehead in sudden realization. 'Burpy's!' She twisted round to face her pals, who were looking at her bewildered. 'Remember Tiara told us Burpy will have a record of everyone who bought costumes there. If we can get a look at those records, we'll find out who's behind the zombie pirate and the curse!'

'You're right!' Olly beamed at her. 'Brandish,' he called up to the driver's seat. 'We need to take a detour to Burpy's!'

'No can do, boy!' Brandish wrenched at his wheel to narrowly avoid an elderly lady with a sausage dog, clutching a steaming bag of chips. 'My orders were to take you all home, and that's what I'm going to do. You'll have to visit Burpy's in the morning.'

Riz sulked but gave a quick nod to her pals in the back seat. 'Tomorrow morning, nine o'clock sharp,' she told them. 'We'll hunt down those records and end this once and for all.'

CHAPTER SIXTEEN

BANG! BANG! BANG!

Riz swam up from the depths of sleep and opened her left eye a crack. The sound of panicked knocking echoed through the house and set the floorboards of her bedroom rattling. She sat up with a start, whacking her head on the shelf above her bed. Early morning sunlight was filtering through the gap in her curtains, setting the ugly pink pattern aglow.

'What's happening?' she muttered to no one in particular.

The banging came again, followed by the shrill ringing of the doorbell.

'Open up! Police!'

The hammering downstairs came again, followed by the sound of her mum's bedroom door bursting open.

Riz swung her legs out of bed and darted to her own door, pressing her ear up against the wood. Downstairs, she heard the key turning in the lock and the front door being wrenched open.

'What is going on?' Mrs Sekhon barked. 'Do you know what time it is?'

'Apologies, ma'am.' Riz stilled at the recognizable voice ... Mayor Turbot was downstairs. 'We need to come in as a matter of extreme urgency!'

Mrs Sekhon muttered something about manners and common decency, but she ushered him and the police inside anyway. Riz strained to listen to his gabbling voice as the kitchen door was opened and then shut again. Then came the sound of the kettle being flicked on.

Riz felt a strange mix of excitement and fear. What on earth could the mayor and the police want with her mum? The kitchen door suddenly opened again, and the sound of her mum's voice carried up the stairs.

'Riz! Can you come down here, please?'

She buried her head in her hands, suddenly worn out. Couldn't she have *one* day off without someone dragging her into trouble? She quickly changed into a T-shirt and jeans and plodded down the stairs.

The mayor looked even more crumpled than usual. His clothes were a mess, his eyes were bloodshot and he paced up and down the kitchen, wringing his hands together as if he was awaiting terrible news. A police officer with the nametag OFFICER SIAN was sitting at the kitchen table, looking grim. She had straight black hair, an even straighter posture and a smile that didn't reach her eyes.

'We just want a quick chat, Riz,' said Officer Sian. 'We've already interviewed your friends Olly Rudd and Drew and Anton Hill. Please take a seat.'

Mrs Sekhon hovered by the kettle, still wrapped in her enormous puffy dressing gown. 'Sit down, love,' she told Riz. 'Talk to them.'

Riz sat opposite the mayor, who had collapsed onto a seat, and was breathing heavily. Officer Sian flipped open her notebook.

'Riz,' Officer Sian began. 'We want to ask you some questions about—'

'WHERE ARE THEY?' Mayor Turbot suddenly shrieked, banging his fist down hard on the table. Officer Sian jumped with fright, almost falling off her chair.

'Where are who?' Riz looked shocked as the mayor buried his head in his hands with an agonized groan.

'Perhaps you should let me handle this, Mayor Turbot.' Officer Sian glanced at him nervously. He whined in agreement.

'Don't I get a phone call?' Riz interrupted. 'I want my phone call!'

'You're not under arrest, sweetie,' Officer Sian told her, talking down to Riz as if she was a four-year-old. 'We're just looking for some information.'

Riz folded her arms like she'd seen criminals do in the TV programme her mum liked about a knitting group who solved gruesome murders in their little English village.

'Riz,' said Officer Sian again, fixing her with an unwavering gaze. 'What do you know about Keith and Judith?'

There was a pause. Riz frowned, not sure if she'd heard the question correctly. 'The eels?'

'Who else?' barked the mayor, lifting his head and glaring at her.

'That's right, the eels.' Officer Sian ignored the outburst and instead stared at Riz, her pen poised over her notebook.

Riz shrugged. 'What about them?'

Officer Sian raised an eyebrow. 'Where were you last night between the hours of midnight and four a.m.?' she asked, a harder tone creeping into her voice now.

'She was here, of course,' Mrs Sekhon jumped in. 'In bed.'

'Can anyone verify that?' asked Officer Sian.

Riz frowned. 'My pillow? What's this all about?'

'Keith and Judith are missing,' said Officer Sian suddenly.

'The eels are missing?' Riz looked from Officer Sian to her mum and then to the mayor, who was blowing his nose loudly into his hankie. 'Since when?'

'Since between midnight and four a.m. last night,' Officer Sian repeated.

'And you think I have them up in my bedroom?' Riz almost laughed, but at Officer Sian's expression the giggle fizzled out in her throat.

The mayor's face was suddenly inches from hers, his eyes wide and wild. 'They've been stolen!' He choked. 'Eel-napped!'

'Today, as you know, is the final day of the Festiv-Eel, where Keith and Judith are released for their annual swim to the Sargasso Sea,' Officer Sian continued. 'We need to know their whereabouts as a matter of urgency. Is there anything you want to share with us, Riz?'

'No!' Riz looked to her mum, who was staring back bewildered. 'I don't know where they are!'

'Nonsense!' snapped the mayor, banging the table again. 'You and your friends have been mixed up in all this since the beginning, spreading lies about curses and treasure and leading my darling Tiara astray!'

'We don't know anything about the eel-napping!' Riz insisted, but no sooner had the words left her mouth than a thought struck her, and she blurted it out. '"The first day brings a salty sea, the next a terrible grip. The third will make you rue the day you laid eyes on my ship." It's just like Huxley's poem said. The same person must be behind the curse, the zombie, the seawater and the krakens!'

'We've heard enough of this.' The mayor stood up and stabbed an accusatory finger at Riz. 'You lot have been rabbiting on about this pirate nonsense for days, and it ends *now*, by order of the mayor!'

Riz jumped up, her face burning red. 'I've had enough of this! I'm sick of me and my friends being blamed and labelled liars!'

'Riz, sit down,' her mum said sternly. 'You don't talk to people like that!'

'I've had it with PEOPLE!' she yelled, turning on her heel and stomping out of the kitchen. She pounded up the stairs to her room, grabbed her rucksack and slung it over her shoulder.

As Riz came back down the stairs, her mum was standing in the hallway. 'Riz, where are you going?'

'Out!' Riz told her, reaching the final step and heading for the front door. She yanked it open and stepped into the fresh air. 'We're going to solve this case, no matter what it takes!'

CHAPTER SEVENTEEN

The clock inside the Snoops Bay bell tower was chiming nine when Riz freewheeled her bike into the town square, looking for her friends. It was deserted, apart from the odd Festiv-Eel flyer skittering along the pavement. The sound of a brass band tuning up floated in from the harbour, along with the clatter and bang of a stage being erected. Somewhere in the distance she heard the mournful wail of a police siren. The town would be waking up to the news that its two star performers were missing.

Riz cast her eyes around and spotted Olly, Drew and Anton hovering under the shade of the huge oak tree, looking more than a little worried.

'So I guess the mayor paid you a visit too?' asked Olly as she pulled up beside them. She gave a grim nod.

'They just announced the news on the radio,' Drew told

her as they chained their bikes up by the tree. 'They're forming search parties down at the harbour. Every police officer in town is on the lookout for two eels.'

As if on cue, a sudden rush of activity erupted out down the street. A crowd of people came marching round the corner. They looked like a hastily assembled search party.

'You four!' barked a police officer, shoving a blurry photograph of Keith and Judith in the friends' faces. 'Have you seen these eels? They're about a metre long, have slimy

skin and answer to the names Keith and Judith?'

The group shook their heads and dodged out of the way of the oncoming crowd.

'Let's move!' hissed Drew. 'We can't waste any more time!'

'This way to Burpy's.' Olly elbowed his way through the throng and disappeared down an alleyway. Riz, Drew and Anton followed.

It only took a few minutes for them to reach the fancy-dress shop, which was proudly wearing a new coat of rainbow paint to celebrate the Festiv-Eel. The window was an explosion of colour with mannequins dressed in gaudy costumes. There was a farmer, a soldier, a zombie, a nun, a zombie nun, a vampire, a werewolf and more, all crammed into the tiny shop window that was festooned with balloons and streamers. But there was no sign of life. The upstairs curtains were tightly drawn, and the CLOSED sign above the door swung eerily in the morning breeze.

Anton pressed his face up against the glass and peered in. 'No sign of Burpy!'

'What now?' hissed Olly, casting a nervous glance back up the street where the sound of the searching crowds was getting louder.

Drew pressed down on the door handle and his eyes widened in disbelief. 'I think someone else has been here.'

The handle had come away in Drew's hand, clearly broken by the last person to enter the shop. Someone had badly wanted a costume, it seemed.

Anton stared at the door nervously. 'I think we should get the police.'

Drew ignored him and gave the door a hard shove. It flew open with a thud, and he looked back with a shrug. 'I don't think anyone's home.'

'This is breaking and entering!' squeaked Anton, looking scandalized.

'We're not breaking if it's already broken!' Drew shot back. 'We're just entering!'

At that moment, a crowd of people appeared at the top of the street, making their way down towards the children. 'KEITH! JUDITH!' someone was shouting. 'WHERE ARE YOU?'

'Inside!' hissed Riz, elbowing Anton and Olly through the doorway before following Drew into the gloom. She shut the door softly behind them, and the noise of the approaching crowd fell to a low murmur.

Burpy's was a very strange place when it was empty.

Mannequins seemed to fill every square centimetre, giving the impression of a crowded room, but it was lifeless. The blank eyes of the dummies stared straight through the children as they made their way deeper inside.

A long counter ran the entire length of the shop, packed with boxes of fake moustaches, enormous comedy glasses, plastic ears, practical jokes and birthday cards. The shelves behind the counter groaned under the weight of wigs and masks, wrapped tightly in plastic, and the children had to stoop slightly so as not to collide with the flowing frocks and ghoulish costumes that hung from the ceiling. Everywhere they looked another set of eyes stared at them.

'What now?' whispered Anton, wincing at the odour. 'This place gives me the creeps! And where's Burpy?'

'Probably off searching for Keith and Judith,' muttered Riz, picking her way past an overflowing bin of Viking helmets. 'Let's find his records!'

Drew hopped neatly over the counter and began to paw through the piles of notebooks and receipts under the cash register. 'Burpy really needs a better organization system.' He tutted. 'This place is a mess!'

'Check the drawers too,' Riz urged him, ducking

down low in fright as the search party passed outside the window. 'And hurry up!'

Drew disappeared under the counter, muttering to himself as he rifled through the drawers. 'GOT IT!' He reappeared, beaming and clutching a thick ledger that had the title SALES RECORDS printed across the cover.

Suddenly, a scream reverberated around the room.

Riz, Olly and Drew whipped round to see Anton pointing a trembling finger into the gloom of the shop.

'IT'S HUXLEY!' he yelled.

CHAPTER EIGHTEEN

Olly pulled Anton back, squinting into the darkness. A wave of relief swept over him, and he found himself laughing.

'Calm down, Anton,' he sighed. 'It's only a costume!'

And so it was. Standing in the corner of the shop, keeping guard over a rotting old wooden chest, was the figure Riz and Drew had seen on the *Captain's Revenge*. Riz pushed past the two boys and inspected it. It was exactly how she remembered – two fiery-looking eyes leering out at her and skin that was rotten and curling away from the skull. But now that she could see the costume up close, she noticed the imperfections. The decaying teeth looked like plastic, and the stringy hair smelled strongly of rubber.

'I can't believe I fell for this.' She shook her head and

turned away from the dummy.

Anton gave it a gentle prod and shuddered. 'I still don't like it.'

Drew had just about recovered from the shock of Anton's shout and turned back to Burpy's sales records. He began to turn the pages, but his face quickly fell. 'It's gone!' he looked up, panicked. 'The whole of last week's records have been ripped out!'

'Someone got here before us.' Olly kicked at the Viking helmet bin in frustration. 'They must have broken in and removed the record to cover their tracks!'

Riz buried her head in her hands. 'Think,' she muttered to herself. 'There must be something we're missing!'

'Who would have known we were coming here?' Drew tossed the ledger to the floor in disgust.

'What's that?' Olly was staring at a small scrunched-up ball by Riz's feet. He crouched down and plucked it off the dusty floorboards.

'What's what?' Anton was still staring at the dummy of the zombie pirate. It stared back at him.

Olly smoothed out the ball and peered down. 'It's a photograph from the opening day of the Festiv-Eel,' he breathed, a quiver of excitement entering his voice.

'During the Pufferfish Puff-Off competition.'

Drew suddenly stiffened. He leapt back across the counter and dived over to where Olly was standing. 'I overheard Tiara complaining at the aquarium that she was missing photos from that day. What if this is one of them?'

Olly dropped the photo to the floor. He turned to his friends as an awful realization dawned on his face.

'It is. Tiara didn't realize it at the time, but her camera caught our culprit red-handed as he poured seawater into the iced tea.'

'Guys …' came Anton's voice, high pitched and trembling.

'Caught who?' Drew clawed the photograph from the floor to see for himself.

'WHO?' yelled Riz.

'Guys …' Anton said again. 'Huxley just blinked at me.'

Silence filled the air.

Olly swivelled his head to face his friend. 'What did you say?'

In one explosive flourish, the zombie pirate burst into life. It grabbed hold of Anton tightly, who howled in terror and clawed wildly at the zombie's face.

'What clever little clams you are!' The zombie grinned.

Riz, Olly, Drew and Anton watched in shock as the zombie raised a barnacle-encrusted hand and whipped off its mask.

'What clever little clams, indeed!' growled Captain Jasper Brandish.

The children stood speechless and slack-jawed in astonishment. His face seemed to have shifted – only slightly, but he no longer wore the expression of a weary old sea captain fed up with the world and everyone in it. His lip curled slightly upwards, and two narrowed eyes peered out at them under his arched eyebrows. He glanced at a shelf at the very back of the room, before saying, 'Aren't they clever, Kourtney?' The children craned their necks and immediately spotted the fishbowl tucked away in the corner with a smug-looking Kourtney swimming around inside.

'You . . .' Riz grimaced. 'It was you this whole time!'

'It took you long enough to figure it out!' Brandish grinned. As quick as a flash, his hand leapt to his belt, and with a great flourish, he pulled a frozen swordfish from beneath the costume and jabbed it in their direction. 'Nobody move!' he barked.

The friends froze. Brandish pushed Anton roughly away, and with the speed of a cat, he moved between the children and the door. He lowered the swordfish slightly but kept a tight grip on its tail.

'I told you to stay away from Huxley's ship, didn't I? But you four little busybodies couldn't help yourselves. You had to have a share of the treasure for yourself!'

'You're the one who wants the treasure!' Drew shot back.

Riz glared at Brandish. 'So Mayor Turbot, Squid O'Malley and Tiara had nothing to do with this? It was all you, trying to scare the town so they'd keep away from the ship and the treasure?'

Memories from the Festiv-Eel suddenly replayed in Riz's mind. Brandish listening intently to their story about finding the *Captain's Revenge*. Brandish sopping wet outside Burpy Gumby's just after their encounter with the zombie, claiming he had been chasing a lobster in the pool. Brandish ladling out iced tea at the Pufferfish Puff-Off, where he was snapped by Tiara's camera. Brandish slipping a sea bass into Tiara's bag outside the aquarium, as she showed off her *GossWorld* article to them.

'I can't believe you were the zombie on the ship that day.' Riz glared at Brandish with furious venom, as if she could explode him into smithereens with just the power of her eyes.

'I'm Burpy Gumby's best customer.' He gave a little titter. 'Apart from that idiotic Turbot girl.'

'It was you that left the receipt at the ship,' Drew said as the pieces of the puzzle fell into place. 'We thought there were three people there that day, but there was one and a blobfish on a skateboard. And you were the only one who knew we were coming to Burpy's this morning, so of course you came to get rid of the evidence.'

From her bowl, Kourtney gave a cackling gurgle. Brandish took a step towards the group, raising his swordfish again.

'So who are you?' Riz demanded, glancing at the door behind Brandish. If they could keep him talking, maybe he'd let his guard (and the swordfish) down so they could make a run for it.

'Someone who has an interest in buried treasure,' he snapped. 'That's all you need to know, twerp!'

Olly narrowed his eyes, clenching his hands into fists.

'There's no treasure on that ship,' Drew told Brandish. 'It's a made-up story, just like Captain Horatio Huxley's curse.'

A grin flickered over Brandish's face before hardening and settling into place as he raised his swordfish again. 'That is where you are quite mistaken, boy.' He stepped aside, tipping his head towards the chest in the corner of the room where he'd just been standing. 'See for yourself!'

The four of them leant cautiously in to take a closer look.

'What is that . . . ?' Olly muttered.

'It's what Huxley took to the bottom of the ocean centuries ago,' Brandish purred.

Olly gave a gasp and Brandish chuckled again. 'Keith's and Judith's eel-napping served as the perfect diversion, you see,' he continued. 'I needed to get the police away from the *Captain's Revenge*, so I decided to *borrow* Keith and Judith. Then I took another trip down to Bony Beach – one more treasure hunt, for old times' sake. And look what Captain Jasper Brandish found under the floorboards of Huxley's cabin . . .'

The group stared at the chest, a weathered and beaten old thing about the size of a large suitcase. Hard shells and

limpets clung to the lid, and it was covered by a dusting of salt crystals, stains from the long-evaporated seawater. Two stout letters had been engraved directly under the lock, although they were now almost invisible: H.H.

'Horatio Huxley's gold. The treasure chest of the *Captain's Revenge*!' crowed Brandish.

'It's real!' gasped Anton, gazing wide-eyed at his brother.

'Oh, it's *very* real,' Brandish told him. 'And the gold inside it is real too ... once I work out how to get to it.' He scowled. 'The lock is rusty, to say the least.' The smile washed off his face and he gestured to Drew and Olly with the swordfish. 'You two, bring the chest over here now!'

Drew and Olly reluctantly heaved the chest towards Brandish. Olly's legs buckled for a moment, and it almost plummeted from his grasp.

'Careful!' hissed Brandish.

'When are you going to let us go?' Anton demanded. 'Our parents will be looking for us!'

Brandish swiped the swordfish in his direction. 'Button it, boy! Kourtney and I will be long gone before anyone gets here!'

He suddenly fell silent as there was a sound outside the shop.

'Burpy?' It was Tiara Turbot. She cupped her hands round her eyes as she peered through the window. 'Burpy? Are you in there? I need to see your sales records!'

CHAPTER NINETEEN

Brandish pulled Riz towards him, poking her in the back with the tip of the swordfish's nose. He pressed a finger to his pursed lips. Nobody moved.

'Don't say a word!' whispered Brandish.

'Hellooo,' called Tiara, her voice growing louder. 'Open up, Burpy!'

Olly locked eyes with Riz, and she looked back at him questioningly. He glanced at the swordfish, his head tilting ever so slightly downwards, and then to Brandish. The captain's eyes were fixed on the door, listening hard to Tiara's voice outside. Olly's eyes drilled into Riz's, trying desperately to communicate. She looked back down at the swordfish and smiled.

'Hello?' Tiara called again, sounding a bit less sure of herself. 'Is there anybody in there?'

Riz took a breath and nodded at Olly.

Three, two, one . . .

'WE'RE IN HERE!' they bellowed. 'HEEEEELP!'

Brandish's eyes bulged with shock. 'SHUT IT!'

'Who's in there?' The door suddenly burst open, and there stood Tiara, staring wide-eyed into the gloom of the shop. Riz gritted her teeth and grabbed the swordfish's nose. She tugged it from Brandish's grasp and swung it at his head, connecting cleanly with his temple. He yelled out in pain and recoiled, straightening up just in time to receive another hard blow to the ribs.

'OUCH!' he wailed. 'THAT HURT!'

Anton leapt towards the door. 'Tiara! Get out of here!'

'GO!' yelled Riz at her friends, ducking as Brandish staggered towards her. 'RUN!'

They dashed towards Tiara, who was standing in the doorway, flabbergasted.

'No time to explain!' Olly told her, grabbing Tiara by the arm and pulling her back out of the shop.

'COME BACK HERE!' spluttered Brandish, as Riz gave him another hard whack with the swordfish on her way out.

'Fat chance!' shouted Drew. The five of them dashed

into the fresh air, the sound of the crowds in the square filling their ears.

'Will someone please tell me what's going—'

A whizzing sound interrupted Tiara, followed by a *thunk* as a streetlight above them exploded. Another *thunk* quickly followed, this time coming from the shop door. A frozen starfish was embedded in the glass, cracks spidering out around it. The children whipped back round and saw Brandish barrelling through the shop towards them, his eyes narrowing to slits as he aimed more frozen seafood at them.

Tiara suddenly shoved Riz out of the way. 'GO!'

Thunk!

She gave a startled splutter, keeling over and landing in Riz's arms. Tiara moaned, her hands scrabbling at her back pocket. A starfish was sticking out of her rump.

'Tiara!' gasped Riz. 'Are you hurt?'

With another groan, Tiara yanked the starfish from her backside, gazing at it in amazement. 'I don't think so ...' she began, plunging her hand into her back pocket. Her look of shock turned to a giggle as she pulled out her thick pink notebook. The starfish had left a deep dent in the very centre of the leather cover.

'Well, would you look at that.' Tiara beamed at Riz. 'Journalism saves lives!'

In spite of herself, Riz laughed.

The crowd was now gathering outside the shop, drawn by the commotion.

'Let me through! Let me through, I say!' Mayor Turbot suddenly thrust his way out of the mass of people. He was soaked in sweat, as if he'd personally combed the seabed for Keith and Judith. His eyes fell upon his daughter. 'Tiara!' he squawked, doubling over and gripping his knees for support. 'What on earth have they done to you?'

Riz took a step back, raising her hands in self-defence. 'Mayor Turbot, you have to listen to me.'

'SQUID!' bellowed the mayor, frantically beckoning into the crowd. 'That little troublemaker and her friends are here.'

The crowd of curious onlookers suddenly parted, shrinking away as a furious-looking Squid O'Malley strode forward. She glared at the children and ripped off her fedora, sending it flying.

'No sudden movements, you five!' she growled. 'I want my eels back. And I have a feeling you know where they are!' With her final word, she pulled a whip from her belt and cracked it hard in the air.

'It wasn't us!' Olly stepped in front of Riz, shielding her with an arm. 'It was Captain Jasper Brandish! He took Keith and Judith!'

'What's all this nonsense?' spluttered Mayor Turbot, looking like he might pop with exhaustion.

'It's true!' Drew pointed back into the fancy dress shop. 'He told us he took them to lead the police away from the ship so he could find Captain Huxley's treasure!'

'Rubbish!' the mayor snapped. 'How many times do I have to tell—'

Mayor Turbot's words died in his throat. A low rumble had started up, making the pavement vibrate.

'Is that an engine?' said Squid, lowering her whip slightly.

The sound was coming from inside Burpy's. The five children turned slowly and began to back away, unsure of what was about to emerge from the gloom inside.

Squid took a tentative step forward, as if she was walking on quicksand. She cocked her head to one side, listening hard.

'A boat engine?' she questioned.

'Hello?' the mayor approached the door, pushing past the group. 'Captain Brandish, is that you?'

With an almighty crash, the front window of the shop exploded outwards, showering the street with glass and sending the crowd scattering for cover. The roar of an engine followed. Brandish was riding a skateboard – Kourtney's skateboard – but it didn't look like it had before. An enormous motor had been strapped to its rear end, belching plumes of black smoke as Brandish soared through the air and skidded onto the pavement. With a triumphant cackle, he whipped round to face the crowd. Huxley's treasure chest was slung on his back, which strained under a pair of knotted straps.

'BRANDISH!' Mayor Turbot flung himself to the ground to avoid being struck head on by the skateboard. 'What on earth are you doing?'

Brandish hoisted the chest higher onto his back and gunned his engine. 'You should have listened to the brats!' he shouted over the roar. 'Later, losers!'

He wrenched the handle of the motor down, and the skateboard shot forward with an ear-splitting rumble. It barrelled up the hill, as onlookers shrieked in fright and dived out of its way.

Squid clambered to her feet, a dazed look on her face. Her whips lay all over the street like stunned snakes.

'He's getting away!' yelled Olly, who was staring dumbfounded up the hill. 'Stop him!'

The wail of a siren cut through the chaos. Up the hill, a few hundred metres ahead of Brandish, a squad car careered round the corner. Through the windscreen, Riz could just about make out the face of Officer Sian, bent grimly over the wheel.

Brandish saw the squad car at the same time as everybody else did. He wrenched the lever of his motor and twisted his body, curling back round and powering down the hill towards the crowd. His face was twisted into a determined snarl as he leant forward, teeth bared in the wind.

'Get back!' yelled Mayor Turbot, flattening himself against the shopfront. 'Everyone, get out of the way!'

Riz, who was staring at the scene in horror, suddenly felt a hand shake her shoulder. Anton was by her side, thrusting something at her.

'Quick!' he yelled over the roar of the approaching skateboard. 'Grab this!'

Riz looked down at what he'd bundled into her palm. It was a collection of Squid's whips knotted together. She stared at it for a moment, then looked back up to Anton, a grin blooming on her face. 'The streetlight!' she shouted.

Anton darted across the street, crouching low under the shattered bulb. Riz ran to the streetlight directly opposite, trusting herself to stay still until the perfect moment. She dropped to her knees and locked eyes with Anton.

Brandish had almost reached them, and he was close enough now for Riz to see the spittle spraying from his mouth as he let loose another laugh. He gave a mock salute to Mayor Turbot as he approached. 'So long, maaayyoooorrrr!' he called, flying past.

'NOW!' yelled Riz.

In perfect unison, she and Anton stood up, pulling their whip-rope taut and tying it fast to the pole of each streetlight. Riz didn't have time to do a double-knot – she just had to pray it would hold.

Brandish saw the barrier in the path of his skateboard a second too late. His mouth formed a tiny 'o' of shock and a moment later he hit the rope. The skateboard carried on, flying off down the hill and towards the harbour before disappearing from sight. But the captain wasn't on it. Like an enormous rubber band stretched to breaking point, the rope gathered Brandish up in its embrace, then spat him back with a ferocious *twang*. With a squeal, the blur that was Brandish sailed through the air and landed with a crunch on the pavement.

'Ooof!' Olly winced at the sound. 'That had to hurt.'

Riz found herself hurrying to the spot where Brandish had landed, ignoring the shouts of the mayor to stay away. She stopped dead. He was moving!

Brandish raised his head slightly with a groan. 'I'm going to need some paracetamol,' he whined.

The impact should have broken every bone in Brandish's body. Instead, the treasure chest strapped to

his back seemed to have cushioned him. But the chest itself hadn't survived the crash, and it now lay split open, pouring its contents onto the street.

Riz looked down in amazement. 'You've got to be joking.'

CHAPTER TWENTY

Once again, the four friends found themselves at Olly's, listening to his report about the recent events in Snoops Bay. This time they were in the garden, slurping on eel-shaped ice lollies.

Olly was standing up, reading aloud from a sheaf of paper still hot from the printer in his parents' office. Drew and Anton lay on their backs, eyes closed in the sunshine. Anton let out a little snore, and Riz prodded him sternly.

'*The police found Keith and Judith snoozing in one of the tanks in Brandish's flat,*' Olly continued reading, '*not seeming the least bit bothered by all the panic their disappearance had caused. By the time the two eels had had a bite to eat and were transported down to the harbour, the sun had begun to tickle the horizon, sending orange and red light giggling across the surface of the sea.*'

'Giggling?' Drew raised his head, frowning. 'Sunshine doesn't giggle, Olly.'

'I was being creative,' Olly told him with a frown. 'I think it works quite nicely.'

Drew shrugged, raising an eyebrow at Riz.

Olly read on. *'Hundreds of people were waiting eagerly for the big moment when Keith and Judith would be released into the sea. Snoops Bay's finest eel-trainer, Squid O'Malley, was in attendance. She was joined by Mayor Turbot, who wished Keith and Judith the best ahead of their newest adventure.'*

'I think I've had enough adventures to last a lifetime,' muttered Riz.

Olly cleared his throat loudly. *'Squid raised her whip and cracked it triumphantly as the crowd cheered. The shape of two eels shot through the air, somersaulting in front of the huge yellow sun and plunging down into the waves of Snoops Bay harbour. There was a spurt of foam, a flash of wriggling bodies and then Keith and Judith were gone – leaving behind the joyous roar of the audience and the shrieking of fireworks.'*

'Beautifully written, Olly,' Riz told him, giving him a little round of applause.

He smiled and continued happily. *'As you, dear reader, have now probably guessed, Captain Jasper Brandish was not a sea captain. His name wasn't even Jasper Brandish. According to Officer Sian, police found dozens of passports in a box under his bed. His real name is Simon Scripps, a second-hand ironing board salesman from Dorkney. Officer Sian says there's over a hundred arrest warrants out for him under different names for fraud, burglary and unpaid parking tickets. He moved to Snoops Bay five years ago, set up shop in the Red Herring, and created a new life for himself as a salty old sea dog under a false identity.'* Anton shook his head, scandalized. *'Scripps is now in police custody and is receiving treatment for a bad case of whiplash.'*

'Literally whiplash.' Drew snorted and winked at Riz and Anton as Olly folded up his article and stowed it proudly in his front pocket.

Olly closed his eyes for a moment and felt the heat of the sun on his eyelids as he allowed a smile to creep across his face. The chest had contained no treasure whatsoever. Instead, the street had been strewn with mounds of dirty washing – moth-eaten pants, rotten old stockings and ragged undershirts. Captain Horatio Huxley and his crew clearly hadn't cared much about laundry.

Simon Scripps had wailed in despair when he caught sight of the mess. 'No!' he'd yelped as Officer Sian clamped a pair of handcuffs round his wrists and hauled him towards her police car. 'Where's my gold and silver?'

'Looks more like grimy old socks.' Olly had giggled, prodding a stained pair of underpants with his toe.

Olly chuckled again now just thinking about it. He opened his eyes and spotted the top of a fedora hat over the garden wall. 'Squid, is that you?'

Squid O'Malley had entered through the garden gates

and was ambling towards them. 'Hello, you four! I was just on my way to grab dinner,' she told them. 'Fish and chips, I think.'

'Hiya, Squid. Do you miss Keith and Judith?' Anton propped himself up on his elbows and gazed up at her.

'A little,' she admitted. 'They'll be just off the coast of Ireland now, paying a visit to the dolphins in Dingle.'

Riz glanced at Olly. He noticed and cleared his throat.

'We owe you an apology, Squid,' he said quietly.

'Oh?' Squid lowered herself onto the grass, plucking off her hat and laying it carefully in her lap.

'At one point we thought you were behind the ship's curse,' Olly admitted, avoiding her gaze. 'And that it was you hunting for the treasure.'

Squid shrugged. 'Well, I owe you all an apology too. Scripps had me well and truly fooled – a conman living under our noses all this time. I suppose he was waiting for the perfect scam to come along.'

'And then we found the *Captain's Revenge* ...' Riz muttered to herself.

Squid nodded. 'I suppose he couldn't help himself, knowing there was long-lost treasure waiting to be discovered. Old habits die hard. Some people are born to be con artists, just like others are born to be eel-trainers. And some are born to be journalists!' She winked at Olly.

'Speaking of journalists.' Over the wall, Drew spotted Tiara Turbot walking by, carrying something round under her arm.

'Tiara!' called Drew. 'Come say hi!'

Tiara seemed to hesitate for a moment, before joining them in the garden. Her face was red and she nervously cleared her throat.

'Spit it out, lass,' said Squid, not unkindly.

Tiara straightened up and looked around at the friends. 'I thought you four did a brilliant job of catching Captain ... I mean, Simon Scripps. And thank you for rescuing me from the kraken, Riz. That was very brave of you. You're all right, all of you.'

Riz glanced at her friends, then back up at Tiara. Her face broke into a wide smile. 'You're welcome, Tiara,' she said. 'Thank you for coming to our rescue at Burpy's.'

Tiara allowed herself a smile and gave a little salute, nearly dropping the fishbowl.

'Is that who I think it is?' Squid leant over and peered into the bowl.

It sure was. Kourtney the blobfish stared out at the

group, looking as sad and dejected as ever. She sighed and burbled out a few bubbles.

'This one is going straight to jail!' Tiara told them. 'Well, a fish tank in a prison warden's office. She was an accomplice to fraud after all.'

'Oh.' Anton frowned, staring at Kourtney's sad eyes. 'I feel a bit sorry for her. She'll be miserable there,' he said, looking to Squid who shrugged.

'She's always miserable,' she told him. 'It's her saggy little mouth!'

Olly suddenly sat bolt upright and grabbed his rucksack. 'Hang on. We can do something about that. Remember the false teeth we found when we collected that muck from the *Captain's Revenge*?' The others watched in bewilderment as Olly pulled his treasure tin from his bag and flipped it open. 'Here – this might do the trick!' He carefully dangled the false teeth over Kourtney's bowl then let them fall in with a gentle *plop*. She watched suspiciously as the teeth floated towards her and settled onto the gravel that carpeted her bowl.

'Go on!' Anton gave the bowl a tap. 'Have a try!'

Kourtney seemed to glance at Anton, and then at the teeth. She sidled up to them, investigating the new feature in her home. Then, with an enormous gulp, she stretched open her mouth and wrapped it round the teeth. Turning back to face the group, Kourtney was transformed, a huge set of mucky teeth now sitting happily in the middle of her face.

'She looks delighted!' Riz snorted, and everyone collapsed into laughter at the sight of such a happy blobfish.

'Okay, Kourtney,' sighed Tiara, straightening up. 'Time to send you to prison.' She gave another quick salute and then left the garden. Kourtney swivelled in her bowl and beamed back at the friends.

'What's going to happen to the *Captain's Revenge* now?' Drew asked Squid, who raised her eyebrows.

'I hope they send it back to the bottom of the ocean,' she told him. 'That's if Mayor Turbot doesn't manage to make it his next tourist attraction!'

Riz watched Tiara and Kourtney make their way up the street. For a split second, she saw a flash of something bright in Kourtney's mouth, catching the sun. Squinting, Riz could have sworn she was looking at a gold tooth. Lots of gold teeth. But surely not?

'What about the treasure?' Olly asked, looking stricken. 'All that gold. It might still be on the ship.'

Squid shrugged. 'I think that maybe, just maybe, some treasure is better off staying buried.'

The sunray moved on and the dazzle from Kourtney's grin faded just as quickly as it had appeared. But Riz knew she'd seen what she'd seen.

She looked at Squid, and then at her friends. 'You know what? I think you might be right, Squid.' She grinned in the warmth of the evening breeze. 'I think you might be right.'

ACKNOWLEDGEMENTS

I expected my second adventure with Riz, Olly, Drew and Anton to be an easier ride than my first, *The Case of the Runaway Brain*. Spoiler alert: it wasn't. I had the tremendous privilege of meeting young readers all throughout 2022, which was wonderful, but suddenly I wasn't writing for an imagined readership any more. Instead, I was writing for the countless children who blew me away with their love for my book and my characters. Luckily, the astonishing support from my friends, family and total strangers was immensely reassuring.

Firstly, I must once again give thanks to my agent, Lydia Silver. This year, Lydia has proven herself to be not just a faithful and forensic agent, but also tremendously good company, along with Clare Wallace and her colleagues at Darley Anderson. Thank you all.

My editor, Amina Youssef, has, once again, been invaluable in bringing this story into the world. She's worked tirelessly as a captain, steering this ship into port – though she's much more friendly than Captain Huxley, I promise. Thank you to Amina and all her colleagues at Simon & Schuster Children's Books, who have given me some of my most cherished memories of the last twelve months on the festival circuit.

It's a magical experience to see your words and characters come to life through illustration. David O'Connell has breathed life into these characters with laugh-out-loud wit and quiet brilliance, and for that I'm profoundly grateful. Thank you, David.

Thanks also to Anna Bowles and Leena Lane for their work in bringing fluency and flow to this book. It's greatly appreciated.

To the teachers, parents, librarians, booksellers and festival staff who have given me such a warm welcome to your various events and classrooms throughout the year, sincere thanks. It's humbling to witness the work that you do. A very special thanks to Theresa Kelly, Laura Carey, James McDermott and Amy Devereux for their support of my books.

My BBC family have tolerated and encouraged me every step of the way as I continue my journey through children's fiction. Among them: Chris Clements, Ammie Sekhon, Dom Howell, Kirsty Lackie, Julie Heekin, Shiv Dunn, Laura McGhie, Fraser Wilson, Connor Gillies, Davy Wallace Lockhart, Liam Weir, Annie McGuire, John Beattie, Martin Graham, Judith Ralston and Mags McGeachy. Many thanks to you all.

Thanks too to my colleagues and friends at the University of the West of Scotland, especially Elizabeth McLaughlin, David Scott, Paul Tucker and the indispensable David Allan.

Thank you to all the pals who have given me constant advice and support: Fiona Stalker, Leah Stalker, Cat MacKinnon, Robbie Armstrong, Franchesca Hashemi, Derek O'Brien, Liz Cooney, David Atkinson, Nathan Jackson, Róisín Treacy, Valerie Loftus, Sam Griffin, Nicky Ryan, Andrew Lennon, Ciarán O'Connor, Leah Kieran, Colin Stone, Sarah McMullan, Derek McLaughlin, Emma Cameron, Steph Docherty and Gordon Campbell. Thanks, pals.

To Tracey Hunter, for her hospitality and the wonderful welcome she gave me when I came to her home in beautiful Islay. Thank you, Tracey. Janey, see you for a dance next year.

To those who showed up in such great numbers to welcome *The Case of the Runaway Brain* into the world, thank you. Killian Murphy, Gerry Haugh, Doreen Atkinson, Martin Pender, Teresa Doyle, Peggy Carty, thank you for your support all these years later.

Thankfully, this year I've been able to go home more often to Wexford and Kilkenny. Many of the stories and characters I meet there are beginning to seep into my writing, so I must thank the Kilkenny crowd for their constant warm welcome: John and Trish Ryan, Stephanie, Aoife, JJ, Martin, Cathal and Róisín, Carmel, Richard, Philly and Maureen and many others.

A huge thanks to the calm (mostly) and constant Vanessa Taaffe – a wife, big sister and best buddy all rolled into one. Thank you for everything, Vee.

Lil Chris Ward has again been an enormous support. Thanks, Chris.

Brian and Viv, all my love and thanks to you once again.

Mam and Dad, for your support and wisdom over the

last twelve months – thank you. And, yes, Dad, I'll get the car serviced.

To my godson, Seán. I cannot wait until the day I can crack open one of these books and begin reading it to you. All my love.

And finally, to James Atkinson. This book, my dear friend, is for you.

NICK SHERIDAN

Nick Sheridan is a children's author and award-winning journalist and television presenter, with a decade of experience working in broadcast media. He spent two years reporting and presenting RTE News2day, the young person's news programme for Ireland's national broadcaster, before moving to the main newsroom where he worked on the foreign affairs desk. He then relocated to BBC News Scotland as the Consumer Affairs Correspondent and continues to work for the BBC, presenting television and radio programmes. In his spare time he runs, swims in Scottish lochs and loses pens. His children's books include *Breaking News: How To Tell What's Real From What's Rubbish*, *The Case of the Runaway Brain* and *The Case of the Phantom Treasure*.

HAVE YOU READ?

IS ALSO AVAILABLE TO LISTEN TO AS AN AUDIOBOOK!